The Deception

Beaded Moccasin Chronicles
Book One

Jenai Dawn

ISBN 13: 978-0-692-279748

Many thanks to my Grandmother, my family and beloved friends who inspired me over the years to always write what's in the heart, and share the hardships of our ancestors past as well as the traditions, values and love of family bonds

…. Not yet 16, I stood there before the tribe council. Caught in my web of deceit, I felt as if my world had begun to crumble at my feet.

Nowhere to turn, no true relations left capable of rescuing me from my demise, I felt abandoned by hope.

I was a single mother of an infant, and a secret that could be a blessing or a curse. I was no longer sure of my ultimate fate.

Did anyone know the whole truth? Had they discovered that my son, was the grandson of the most powerful Chief in the region?

I had not spoken a single word to anyone!

No one that had ever been called before the council without there being serious implications. I knew this could not be good!

Chapter 1

I was born Emmalia Rose Littlefoot, on a frigid winter morning in 1911, to a Native American mother in a small tribal village on the south banks of the Pagoda Creek, in Pigeon Gap, Kansas. Frail and much paler than my sister, my mother doted on me and loved me despite how I had come to be a part of her world.

Happiness filled her heart when she held me, and she was content that I had survived being born under such harsh winter conditions with little help of a midwife or nurse maid. No tribes-woman dare assist in helping an infant like me into the world back then. Little did I know or understand the anguish and hardship my existence would bring upon my mother for many years to come.

Not through any fault of her own, but at the cruel hands of an English settler traveling westward, was I conceived in such a brutal manner upon those plains, bringing on such tribulation and shame. Many a soldier who had left the war, and traveled west in search of fortune and land to raise cattle and horses, had left their mark upon the women of our tribes. If they didn't take the women with them, they raped and tortured and left them for dead among the brush, as if they were a discarded carcass after a hunt.

Stories of their snatching women from off of river banks or in fields to be taken and enslaved as mates with whom they could transform into exactly what they wanted, was a fear engrained into the minds of all native women. Even our young girls were at risk of being taken, so they could be brought up in the white man's home and taught the white man's ways. I heard my mother say it was because the white women didn't like to work as hard and some men liked hard workers who they could train to do as they beckoned, and had no family to run home to should they have to beat them into submission. Natives were just savages, and no one cared what happened to them.

My mother was now a widow with two small girls. She had once been married to the brother of our chief. I had a sister who was born two years before me, named Laylah. When I was old enough to know, my mother explained to me that her husband, my sister's father, was killed by a white man, when he tried to defend her honor one spring afternoon.

There was a group passing through the area while the warriors were out hunting who decided to steal our furs, dried meats and rape the women. They attacked with guns and killed anyone who fought against them. Her husband, Laylah's father, was killed, the very same day I was conceived so brutally upon those plains. My mother was scarred with the remnants of the blade that ran across her face, bringing her to submission to the nasty white man's lusts.

~

I grew up among my indigenous people, knowing I was different and frequently being reminded of such by the sneering and scoffs bantered in my direction by the children among the main camp to the north of the creek. Fairer skinned than most, and green eyed, some mocked and avoided being near me, saying my stare bore the image of the "white man's devil within". I learned later, that most of the tribeswomen who had conceived under such circumstances or who had fallen prey to the white man's brutality usually committed suicide, to avoid the shame they felt. I was happy that my mother was not one who felt that way. Despite the circumstances, she felt that every instance in life, good or bad, was the will of the Great Spirit and that life was too precious a gift to sacrifice.

Because of her choice to keep me when she found out she was with child, we were subject to scrutiny and treated differently than the rest of the encampment who survived the raid without harm. Living in the run down south paddock where the chickens, cattle and horses were kept, was tolerable, and we were not alone. We shared our small encampment with several other women who were known as the *reclaimed*.

Among these were a few other women who had been snatched and violated by the white man. Shunned by the tribe and forced to live on the outskirts of the encampments as if they were unworthy, they were destined only to be caretakers or menial laborers for the pure blood among the people.

Several other young girls from nearby tribes were placed to live among us over the past few years when their parents were slaughtered during the many battles that raged between the white men and us. Someone had to care for the little ones who had become parentless victims with no families to look after them. Yet they could not be placed among the main camps for fear of the mental scarring from brutality of the white man's hand bringing bad Spirit and evil to the tribal elders.

Although our lives were not as well-off as the pure-blood that lived on the north side of the creek, we still filled our youthful days with laughter and adventures every chance we got. All tribal children were raised to work hard and waste little time with idle play, until chores were completed. We were subject to harsher labor than the main camp as a means of repayment to the tribe and warriors who fought to keep us from being killed or drug off to some white man's missionary camp to be reformed of our savage ways and beliefs. We must spend a lifetime in servitude for those who sacrificed their lives to save us from our fate.

On occasion, we had the opportunity to play with some of the broken carved toys or handmade dolls discarded by the children of the tribal elders as we sat by the evening fire and our mother's told us stories of the Great Spirit and ancestors past. I loved listening to the stories of the many adventures along the plains before this so-called "white man had come to destroy the beauty that Mother Earth had bestowed our people", as momma would put it bluntly.

Sometimes we would even be privileged to old magazines and catalogs found discarded along the wagon trails made by the white man's families as they traveled westward to take more of our lands. Such a travesty sometimes to see the disrespect for Mother Earth in the deep ruts the noisy wagons made that filled with muddy water when it rained and grew hard and ugly in the cold months. The many fires they did not extinguish when they broke up their camps being carried into the brush by winds, searing natures beauty to mere ash. The remnants resembling discarded rubbish and waste so repulsive, that if the ground could regurgitate and spew them clean out to the ocean in revolt, she would.

Filled with so many emotions as to the white man, and the hatred our tribe held for them, I was unsure how I should feel. Part of this white man's blood was in me! Would I ever one day disrespect the beauty of nature as they did?

Momma said I was a caring child full of love and life and destructiveness would never be a part of my world, and not to fret. She also warned I should never take notice to their flashy trinkets and things they bore, because it was their way of hiding the evil within them. She said, "I was a precious gift to her' and knew she would try her hardest to not let me become what existed as the darker half of me. At the same time I thought often;

How could she, or anyone for that matter, truly love me, as she did my sister, since I was half of that evil after all?

Why couldn't I love the good half of me, despite half of what we were taught to hate so much was me?

How could anyone love me, a half-blood?

~

I continued to gaze upon page after page of pretty pictures of corsets and dresses worn by the white women, as I rested propped against that old birch tree next to the creek that chilly Saturday afternoon. I had found the catalog in some remnants of a camp near where we picked berries a few days back and had hid it in the hollow at the bottom of the tree. The pictures were plain black and white, yet as I glanced at the wonderful fall colors in the trees around me. My thoughts began to wander as my mind drew images of color and lace.

I could see dresses of bright yellows, oranges, or browns like the leaves of the hickory and birch trees. Trimmed with satin and bows of red and purple, like the maple and dogwood leaves, all aching to loft their way down to the earth and replenish her with nutrients before winters cold set in. For now, they graced the branches above me, glistening in the sun, as I sat there lost in thought, dreaming what it would be like to wear such beautiful dresses one day. Surely it had to be much nicer on my flesh than the rough animal hides we were accustomed to wearing. Even nicer than the fancier attire worn by the natives on the north side of the creek for sure!

Now thirteen, I seemed to get caught up in fantasies about a world much different than mine often as a means to escape my reality. One should always listen to the teachings of their parents and their people, my conscience would scoff and remind me often, but it was hard for me to grasp why I felt so different and out of place.

How could our tribe hate the white man so much, for their mean ways, and expect us to honor those who treated us so poorly in our own camp?

Were not our own people just as cruel at times?

Had not the warriors attacked some travelers without provocation, scalped and murdered them just for being white?

I should be listening to the warnings from my mother, to be humble that we were rescued and reclaimed and not forced into the fate of the Plaines alone, but I couldn't share her feelings. I just could not fathom how we could be considered any less brutal and cruel.

Was it really a white man's devil in me that made me feel this way?

What made me wish for some of the white man's things?

What made me desire to want part of their world?

Every chance I had to look through the pictures in those old catalogues and dream of something different, I did. But even more afraid of my mother whipping me for doing so, led me to hide what little treasures they were to me, so as not to have my childish dreams go up in flames some night like we had seen other books and magazines when they were burned.

Some white men, called Missionaries, would bring books full of stories about their God and spiritual ways, hoping we would all learn to believe the same thing and get along. The moment they would leave the camp, our chief would throw them in the fire and chant, hoping to rid the evil Spirit he claimed they harbored, from our midst. He did let the children have the sweet hard things they called 'candy' to eat. *My was it yummy!*

Still I had my doubts and as time passed I dreamed of what it would be like to dance at a grand gathering in such luxury as portrayed in the books, and seen on the traveling missionaries wives. Some of which were designed by people as far away as a place called France. *Oh to be donned in such finery!* I also became quite troubled that perhaps The Great Spirit would punish me for my thoughts. Confused and afraid, I decided I would best survive if I keep my thoughts to myself and focus more on learning to be more pleasing to the Great Spirit and follow my mother's guidance and the ways of our people, and put the white man's world out of my head.

My mother warned me that the Spirit would be unhappy if I kept daydreaming of such frivolity and I knew the Spirit must have somehow ratted me out. Despite being a half-blood, I was nothing more than a "half savage Indian clear to the bone, and I best never forget it", she claimed. "I was to be poor, plain and shunned." She claimed even a white man would treat me like trash and I didn't care. I knew deep in my heart, I was destined for something more. Someday.

I kept that secretly inside my thoughts out of fear of harsh reprimand. The last time I was caught looking at pictures in magazines, my mother whipped my bare bottom so red, that my cheeks looked as if I had been set atop hot rocks to bake. I would not dare get caught again. I had to keep my thoughts silent. Knowing I was destined for something much greater in the future would remain just that, a thought in my head. I just wasn't sure what it was.

Why could I not rid myself of this feeling? Why could I not accept that I was nothing more than a half-blood savage? Was I possessed with some white man's curse? Then I began having weird visions in my sleep and wondered if perhaps it was true, that I had a devil in me!

When I was younger I dreamed that perhaps one day I shall be the bride of a warrior, a hunter, or even a chief. Yet at the same time I questioned whether I would find my way into the white man's world and have the finest gadgetry and beautiful lamps with real glass ornamentation I saw in picture books. Was this just typical teen girl fantasies or was I really possessed with some horrible evil Spirit? I must admit my overactive imagination did tend to run amuck at times, so I was not sure what to think any more. I must be going crazy after all, I thought.

Dreaming was the only means I had to pass the idle evening hours. So perhaps it was my hormone driven brain running wild. I had just begun to show signs of womanhood, that being a horrid curse in itself, why not add demon possession as well? Either way, sometimes my wandering mind became a blessing It helped me forget about the strange voices that invaded my thoughts during the quiet hours of night. I dared never mention the voices to anyone, for surely they would have to put me to death to kill this evil thing within, creating such turmoil.

It was a struggle for me to understand why I always heard these crazy voices or strange dreams at night. Even scarier, when some of the strange dreams and visions I had would come true a few days later!

I remember my mother telling me stories about my elder relatives having gifts, as many Native Americans do. Some would hear voices, that were messages from the Spirit, to be passed on to the tribe, as warnings or blessings of things to come. But not me, I could not be gifted; I am only a half-blood. So I just assumed maybe I was just as crazy as my aunt Mayma. I was just content to not to have random outbursts like her.

Aunt Mayma was often seen talking to animals, trees and rocks as if they were people, and running through the camp near naked, screaming that fire-God's were trying to burn her to death, when she was actually suffering from sunburn. Some days she appeared smart as a whip and others, as loony as if she were maddened by some rabid animal. Momma once told me she was that way after being trampled by horses and had her head cracked clean open, so we made sure not to mock her moments of simple mindedness, for fear of the Spirit becoming angry and afflicting us with something horrible as punishment the likewise.

~

"Emmalia", I heard my mother calling me from a distance. I must have drifted off to sleep that lazy afternoon. The rustling of the fall winds among the changing leaves of the trees and the soothing ripple of the creek waters must have carried me off to a fantasy world again.

I was abruptly awakened from my dream filled state to notice the orange hue of the auburn sun had begun to fade below the hills in the distance and the sky would soon be immense with stars illuminating the night. It was sunset and time to gather the last evening's load of firewood for the main encampment's celebrations that were to commence as soon as the moon was in full view.

Frustrated, I got to my feet and headed into the brush to help gather wood with my sister. Although I was tired of working like a slave to the unappreciative, every moment I spent with my sister was cherished. She never treated me as if I were different. She even stood up for me when other's would treat me unkind. I loved her so much and always enjoyed her being around when there was work to do.

I also knew that one day my sister's future would be blessed with a much better life than we had here. She was a pure-blood and one day, as with other's in the past, she would be moved over to the north side of the creek to be chosen as a bride for a warrior or hunter. But for now, she was with me, and I savored it as much as I could before that time came.

Deep inside, I was secretly jealous of her for being pure blooded, yet sad at the same time wishing that day would never come. I never wanted to separate the bond we had created. I wanted us to share our whole lives together like the rest of the pure-blood sisters did, but the horrific reality was, that would never be.

One day, the time would come and I knew our worlds would part, for now, we were together. Outside of chores, and my moments of daydreaming naps, we were inseparable Since we were not priority for protection by the main camps warriors during the many raids by the soldiers of the government, there were very few of us left in the work camp. Once she was gone, I would have nobody but my mother and aunt.

We were lucky to have survived the many raids. Although I secretly wondered what really would happen if I were to be snatched away and taken to a mission camp of the white preachers. In the same thought, I knew the Spirit would punish me for wanting anything to do with their world. I chose to immediately quashed that horrible image from my mind and took heed to being cautious of the warnings from our people.

I pushed all my wayward thoughts from the day out of my troubled mind and set off hand-in-hand with my sister, singing and laughing as we gathered wood and stuffed our mouths with a few remaining berries left in the bushes nearby. Mouths covered with berry juice and fingers stained a reddish-blue tint, we strode back to the camp, kindling in hand, and happy.

The look on momma's face was not one to be reckoned with! She harshly reprimanded us for silly dawdling and not hurrying to complete our tasks. Momma would also remind us of the dangers of not paying attention to what might be lurking in the woods, and playfulness may lead to our demise. We should always take mind to be alert, she said wearily, as if to know it was spoken in vain.

Well scolded and glad our chores were now completed for the day, we retreated in haste to wash our hands and faces, freeing them of the evidence of our spirited consumption of berries had left behind.

JENAI DAWN

Chapter 2

Drums echoed off the Northern crest of the hills in the distance with a sound so melodic one could almost feel their body pulsate from the rhythm. It was as if it were the beating of Mother Earths heart in tune with the serenading of the gentle breeze that carried the sounds of voices echoing through the night air.

Tonight everyone in the main camp has been busy readying themselves for celebration of the great harvest bestowed upon the people, by nature. The women would now be able to prepare and preserve the gathered crops and the provisions to put up for winter.

The year had been plentiful enough to make sure that no one went hungry in the camps during the harsh winter due to come. Soon there would be even more echoes of dancing, chanting and singing praises to Mother Earth in appreciation as well as homage to the Great Spirit that would last long into the night. That meant much work needed completing to please the Spirit.

There would be a special dance to welcome the Hunters Moon as well. October is so close to winter, the game running wild among the brush and woods have all been fattened through the warmer months and it was now time for the men to go hunting and preparing a store of provisions for the long winter months ahead. Each year plenty of meats and jerky needed to be preserved and kept with the many fruits, nuts and grains harvested.

Young warriors would have their flesh painted with the markings of their accomplishments in previous hunts. This was done to show their stature to the parents of prospective brides and strut around showing their strength and status as they seek out hopeful prospects. The younger boys would sit around the fire and listen to stories and warnings from seasoned hunters as to what will be expected of them when their time comes to partake in the hunt.

~

The women decorated their flesh with colored paints made from berries, clays and plants as well as adorning themselves in their finest dresses which included ornamentation with multiple rows of metal cones and bobbles that created a melodically soothing tune as the dancer swayed to the rhythm of the drums and chants. On other occasions the same type of dresses were worn by the medicine women to dance the healing dance when someone was ill as a means to signal the Great Spirit for them to be possessed with special healing skills to make people well. But not this time. This time it would be in gratitude to Mother Earth for her gifts of plenty.

In preparation for such a glorious affair, my sister and I would spend days washing and cleaning the many beaded and woven mantas worn by the privileged single young women to hang around their dresses, as they presented themselves at the dances in hopes to land the most eligible of bachelors among the hunters seeking to wed.

The dressing up and flaunting usually always took place during the welcoming of the Hunters Moon, so when the hunter was away, his bride could decorate and prepare the home to entertain indoors during the colder months instead of outdoors as done in the warmer months. Another advantage was that he would have someone to prepare his catch and set up the stored goods before the winter freeze.

Such nonsense, I used to think to myself, just to get the attraction of a smelly, sweaty warrior to have to cook for and clean up after. But then I had not really been too interested in being someone's personal slave, unless they could accept me even though I was of mixed-blood.

Some days, when no one was looking we would put on their dresses, spin around, laughing and pretending we were the ones about to be chosen.

As Laylah and I were weary from cleaning some mantas, knowing we would most likely never be privileged to such nice attire, we decided to play around some to perk ourselves up. That was a big mistake! About the time we had just finished a few dance steps and some twirling, we heard a faint succession of thumps on the dirt below our feet.

We glanced down, then raised our heads and stared at each other for a moment in horror. Several beads had fallen off the manta I had wrapped around myself. Laylah gasped and fell to the ground, scurrying to pick them up. "Hush", she rasped quietly as we heard someone drawing close. In a panic she shoved the beads into my moccasins to hide them, just as my mother approached to inquire on what was taking us so long.

It was a good thing she decided to hide the beads quickly in my moccasins, we surely did not want a firm reprimand from our mother. There would be harsh punishment if we were caught being careless or disrespectful to those of higher stature by childish behavior while caring for their belongings.

We hurried off with mother, staying silent about what we had done. We needed to finish preparing the rest of the clothing we were to take to the main camp. We hoped that with sunset taking hold, the owner of the manta would not notice the missing beads in the darkness and just assume they had fallen off during her celebrating.

Not thinking much more of the beads until our chores were done, and my feet were aching from the beads working their way down to the bottom of my moccasin and boring chaffed holes into my ankles, we decided it was time to get rid of the evidence.

We dug a hole in the dirt beneath the

animal skins that were the under sheathing of our bedding of furs in the furthest east corner of our tipi, swearing never to speak of them again. As we dropped each colorful one into the earth, my mind once again wandered to the beautiful colors from the white-mans books, or the pure-bloods from the main camp. I ached to wear something so colorful and pretty. Anything, but the drab garments that donned my now maturing body, adorned only with color painted from the juices of berries and trimmed with whatever feathers I could find from off of the foul that shed them each season.

~

Oh I longed to be one of the maidens who lived among the pure-bloods. I would not be subjected to carrying loads of firewood to a tipi in the dead of winter, chop holes into the ice on the river to collect fresh water, nor would I sweat for so many long hours in the summer heat feeling like a slave to the demands of others. If I were, I would be privy to wearing nice skins adorned with beads just as fancy as the ones now buried for only Mother Earth to see their beauty.

I should not complain really, the women

of the main tribe do work hard in their own way. They just celebrate and party even harder. Something we were never privileged to be included in. Their work was generally respected and honored, for the men knew they could not carry on their lineage without them.

It was considered a great honor to bear and rear many children for a man in the tribe. This ensured that there would be more of our people to pass along our way of life and traditions. Equally as honorable was the women's craftiness in decorating and making their relations lodge or tipis unique in ornamentation and designs as well as a comfortable home for her husband.

In the social standings among the tribe, a household is judged not only by the bravery and generosity of the men, but also by the kindness and care she put into providing for her living quarters. One found honor in cleanliness and decor. I wanted to experience that pleasure, that honor one day.

This skill was passed down by mothers and grandmothers to their daughters. Many a warrior or hunter chose his bride not only by her appearance and status but by how well her mother kept their household, knowing they would have been taught the same skills.

All the lectures on how one was to keep their house one day mattered so little to me, because I was still just a half-blood in other's eyes. I would be doomed to be an old maid, alone until I die like my crazy aunt Mayma, I thought silently to myself.

Listening to the celebration taking place in the distance, aching to belong, yet knowing I most likely never would, I crawled into my bed to slumber for the night. Dreams willing and ready to carry me away from my misery, I fell fast asleep.

~

Weeks had passed and November would come upon us before we knew it. As winter drew closer there would be one more celebration this year before it became too cold to have outdoor gatherings. The grounds that felt the beat of feet dancing and stomping to the beat of drums, would soon be covered in crisp white snow, glistening in the winter sun.

Soon the tribesmen and their families would be settling down with their families in their tipis for the colder months. As we worked and gathered extra wood to store for the winter, we overheard many rumors and whispers around the main camp that Chief Stumblingbear was discontent with the lack of younger maidens to pick from as wives for his son, who still had not chosen a bride.

There were more warriors and hunters than women and they were ready to settle down and marry. They spoke of some considering wanting to marry even late into the winter season possibly, in hopes to bring a new little one into the world by midsummer the following year. The elders were growing troubled that there were not enough women to select from. "They must start choosing from among the camp of the *reclaimed*", the Chief, spoke with a hesitation in his voice.

Although I knew this moment would possibly come one day, I willed it not to exist in my thoughts. Then I gasped under my breath when I heard chief Stumblingbear suggest that perhaps some of the older girls that were of pure-blood could be brought to the main camp from among the reclaimed.

He suggested that the elders must immediately select one and have her prepared for ceremonial marriage, because he would not see his son go another year without a bride that was young enough to bear him many children. 'This must be done within the next day or two", he ordered curtly. I backed up from my secret spot where I had been lurking and listening, and scurried away. I had to get as far from their camp as I could.

Carrying the bundle of kindling in my hands, struggling not to drop any of it in my retreat. I headed to the collection pile, tossed the load down and walked towards the creek, where I always fled to find comfort and silence when troubled, doubting I could find any. My heart was so burdened with the impending doom it felt was about to be lunged my way.

~

"NOOOO... "; my inner voice shrieked, as tears welled up in my eyes, as I thought of the heartache I would feel if this happened. Although I tried hard not to think about it. I knew deep inside that if the Chiefs wishes were upheld, that would mean Laylah could be taken from us! Of course it would be wonderful to see her living among her pure people, but I would lose my best friend, my confidant, the only relations besides my momma and aunt. Both of them were frail. My mother had been growing more feeble since contracting some illness last month, that plagued most of our camp taking many a soul to be with the Spirit, and my aunt was feeble minded most of the time.

I knew if they came to collect my sister I would only be able to see her when I was to gather wood, clean, or do menial chores for the main camp. Being that I was a half-blood I would be considered shunned by her new *family.* Upset this was coming too soon for my liking, I just wanted to be alone. I wanted time to think.

Falling to my knees, in tears on the rocky banks of the creek, I felt as if my heart were burning from the pierce of a flaming arrow. "Please Great Spirit, don't take her from me", I begged aloud.

I sat there soaking my toes in the ice cold water, trying to compose myself, when it began to rain. Part of my subconscious told me, I shouldn't act so jealous and upset but should be rejoicing that she would find a better life and maybe a man who would love her. Yet that was little comfort. It seemed as if the heavens knew my pain and were crying too when the rains began to fall much harder, soaking clean thru my clothing and chilling me clean to the bone. I gathered myself back up as the sky became illuminated with lightning and thunder rumbled fiercely. I needed to make my way back to our tipi for the night before it got any muddier on the path back to camp and my mother would scold me for getting so dirty and climbing into bed a wet muddy mess.

Chapter 3

Just a few more days were left to finish preparations for the dance of the Frost Moon and another celebration with a grand feast. This would be the last celebration before the long winter set in. We spent every waking moment scrounging around like squirrels scurrying to gather nuts for the winter.

There was extra firewood to collect, ceremonial frocks to mend, the last of fruits and berries to pick and herbs to dry and bind for the many smudgings to take place. Not that nature had allowed for many more to be left on branches and in the ground as of late. We had already started having much colder days than this same time last year, and the pickings were slim, but nothing went to waste if we knew a way to dry, preserve or store it.

In three more days it would be the last full moon of the year, called the Frost Moon. This brought on one of the largest celebrations of the year. The tribesmen gathered with their wives and or soon-to-be brides and relations to feast and celebrate. It was a time of singing

31

and dancing songs of praise to the Great Spirit for the wonderful months past though the year and prayers for greater blessings for the upcoming year and to offer up prayers as well for good health and prosperity of the new families starting their journeys together in marriage.

The hunters would spend the next several days setting beaver traps before the creeks froze over for the winter. This was done to ensure a good supply of warm winter furs. Fur trading was becoming something the elders were using as bargaining tools with the white men to keep us in some kind of peaceful status with them.

It was also a celebration as if to say, "farewell" to the warm days of summer and fall and "welcome" to the brutal winters that lay ahead.

I wasn't quite sure how one could find anything that brought on the heavy snow, cold nights and long months of my toes feeling like old man winter had near bit them off, a means to celebrate. I was more inclined to think it had something to do with all the new weddings that took place, and the smug grins on the lucky men who had taken their brides into their homes, some on their second or third by now.

Tradition among our people was whenever there were sisters among relations; when a warrior came and chose his bride; her sisters were also considered future prospects for his household. I didn't think that would ever be a circumstance I had to worry about, since I was a half-blood, and anyone that came to marry my sister one day wouldn't even take a second glance at me. I just hoped that someone would not ignore my sister because she had no siblings to offer in the deal or plans.

Most warriors didn't take the sisters under their roof as a wife until the first wife was about to give birth, and isolated from many activities in her daily life. Her husband would take the next younger sister as a wife to assist with the upkeep of the tipi, the *needs* of the warrior and the birthing of the infant.

I found this ideology quite barbaric. I really did not like the idea of being a slave to some mans needs if I didn't like him.

I clung to the illusion that because I was a half-blood, this would never happen in our household.

I had known the horror stories of how some warriors beat their wives who were not pure, and kept them pent up like dogs, only to be unleashed to perform duties then cast aside like scraps from a skinned bounty from a hunt.

As the time drew closer to the celebration, I felt for sure Laylah was not going to be chosen because we had so little to offer in addition to her. Usually warriors would show signs of interest and that had not happened yet. She was 16 now, no one had come to bring the traditional 'courting' gifts to my mother and our household to show their interest and intent on taking her as a bride, which was our custom in most cases.

Would it be different for us because we were outcasts in a sense?

Would there be no gifts for my mother?

Would they just snatch her anyway?

I had often heard many women saying how in the older days of our ancestors, they felt as if girls were sold, and when I asked my mom about this she said it was kind of the truth but more a misunderstanding of cultural practices.

Tradition was when a young man was considered worthy enough to marry a respectable maiden, both families exchanged presents. However to win the approval of her parents, the young warrior first had to show his worthiness, by showing how generous he could be by sending them some fine horses to ride or other such presents.

Since the parents would be losing such a good household worker, they had to give them something of value in exchange. I tended to agree with what the older women were describing, but my mom said that was how they also knew that the warrior seeking a daughter could afford to provide for her.

I didn't care if the *exchange* was considered a return on an investment in one raising their daughter to her prime and one day marry into the relations of someone of stature. I still thought it was like trading women as if they were like meat to be marketed, and wondered does anyone ever marry for love?

I suppose it didn't matter, it was by far worse to be considered an old maid, like my aunt, who was said to have gone completely mad. She had never been chosen as a bride, and was now looked upon as a crazy and useless slave.

How would a young warrior even show interest in my sister and await the approval of the man of our household, being there was no man in our tipi since my sister's father was murdered by the white man? No one had taken in my mother as their own because of her being tainted by the rape of these evil white men and their ways.

Most women who lost their husbands, were taken in by his siblings, to be looked after. My mother's brother-in-law was the Chief, and his only act of kindness was letting my mother live among the *reclaimed* as a servant, and I hardly call that much compassion and love.

Maybe they would not show this type of tradition in giving of gifts under the circumstances. But I wondered what would be taking place, since I had noticed more of the elders peering at us while we worked lately and whispering among themselves, often pointing to my sister in an eerie way, as if she were a piece of property to be bargaining over. How would they seek out someone from our camp as the Chief demanded? There were only about four teenage girls of marrying age among our camp anyway?

The usual way a young warrior first showed interest and desire for a certain girl was to send a special small gift token to her parents.

I did notice one day that my mother had a new shawl that had been left at the door of our tipi a few weeks back, yet she spoke nothing of it and no one else knew just how it had arrived, nor who had delivered it in the still of the night before.

We just assumed someone felt sorry for my momma and her lack of good health and how the winter months ahead would affect her, and out of compassion left it for her.

Nonetheless, I was too busy gathering and preparing for the celebration to take place in the main camp to think much on the matter. We only had two days left before the celebration and there was much to be done. I was more in fear of reprimand or a caning for not completing tasks expected of me than worrying about the future plans of everyone else. I would have all winter to sit in the tipi and wonder the future and the fate of life happenings to come one day.

I continued to wash clothes and gather wood, prepare fry breads, dry meats, and any other tasks my mother had me do. Baking breads was my favorite domestic task. I had actually become pretty good at baking breads and using the fermented mead from rice to make the bread rise into a nice loaf.

The aroma of all the jellies and breads filled the air with a tantalizing smell that made my mouth water. The best part of celebrations was the times we would sit and enjoy eating all the extra treats made by different women from other tribes close by, when they came to join the celebration at the close of the year and left behind all the excess they didn't want to carry back to their camps late in the night when they left. We would go clean up the main camp and sneak back many of the discarded treats.

Chapter 4

Another too early for me sunrise, and another full day of work to come. My body just ached from all the extra work bestowed upon us to make sure the welcoming of the Frost moon to come in half a day's cycle was inviting to the Spirit and pleasing to the elders of the tribe.

As I crawled out from under my warm bedding, the cold earthen floor below my feet sent a shiver riveting through my tired body, reminding me of just how soon winter would be upon us as well. I slipped my moccasins on my feet, taking time to put extra moss in the bottom and sides in hopes to keep my toes a bit less frosty feeling, then wandered towards the fire, where my sister had already prepared some warm tea for me. Grateful to have such a loving sister who always did such thoughtful things for me, I sat down next to her and with a smile, hugged her good morning and told her how much I loved her. She smiled in return and we sat there silently sipping our tea together, and eating some berry mash on leftover frybread from the evening meal the day before.

My pleasurable morning was quickly interrupted by rustling sounds outside, followed by several male and female voices conversing softly. I couldn't make out what they were saying and as the chatter started fading my sister and I decided we had better get to finishing what was expected of us for the day before we were reprimanded for slacking off.

We bundled up in our shawls and headed outside into the cold morning air. The morning sky had an eerie feeling to it and the dampness in the air felt like it was seeping straight thru the seams of my clothing as each gust of wind crept by.

The sound that disrupted our quiet morning were a few elders walking through our camp and speaking to some of the older women. I would have to inquire of my mother later as to why they were here. Although we were to never question the actions of the elders, nor did I think my mother would say anything anyway, I just felt I had to ask. Something just did not feel right about today. My stomach felt the tension, and I could not shake the feeling of pain that ached in my soul for some strange reason.

I pulled my cloak tighter to try and keep the chill out and sped over to a circle of women sitting around a fire, shelling nuts, and pressing berries, and set my mind to working hard and trying to forget that I felt like a frozen icicle hanging from a branch after a freezing rain pleading to be melted by a hot sun.

The older women kept looking at my sister and me as if we had some sort of plague on our flesh. Whispering on occasion to one another, low enough to not be discernible, I still knew they were talking about one of us, by the way they kept conspicuously peering at us often. It just plain gave me the creeps and atop of being chilled, I began to feel goose bumps all the way from the tips of my toes clean up to my ears. I kept working as fast as I could, and prayed hard to just get finished with my tasks and head somewhere away from everyone.

Nuts all shelled, berries mashed and now firewood collected, dresses mended, and food carried up to the main camp, I headed back down to our smaller camp to see if there was anything I had forgotten to do. Momma said

I was done for the day, and I could go. I went looking for my sister who had gone over to drop things off at another elders tipi, but she had not returned yet. Sighing, and still feeling a bit out of sorts over the day's events and not having her to share my thoughts with, I settled for my usual retreat when I felt displaced.

Sunset was just a few hours away, and I was never so happy to hear momma say I was done working. I could now sneak off to the creek to soak my aching feet in the frosty waters and listen to the sounds coming from the main encampment in the distance as they tightened the skins for the drums and a few whistles from flutes being banded for the events to come very soon.

I enjoyed this moment on the banks of the creek more than usual today. I needed time alone to sort the last few hours of the day. My mother seemed so distant and troubled. I was not sure if it was her health taking a turn for the worse or was there something weighing on her mind that made her seem quite sad today. When the elders from the main camp came visiting, it seemed to have been a bit disconcerting to everyone. It was after all very rare they bothered to come down. Usually if there were something extra they needed from us laborers, they would send just one warrior or woman to request a presence at one of the elders tipis to discuss the needs, then it would be relayed to us later upon their return. It seemed their visit made all of us out of sorts today.

All I wanted to do was just to soak my feet, and try to forget all the work we did, as well as try to forget the jealousy I held deep inside for all the festivities everyone else was to participate in when we did all the work.

Part of me was still so angry that the only glimpses we had of the celebration would be when my mother drifted off to sleep and we could sneak through the creek bed, and hide in the bushes and watch. *If momma knew what we did, she would surely skin us alive!*

In the darkness we would wait in hopes to snatch a morsel of some of the fine scraps discarded when all had succumbed to drunkenness and wouldn't notice us pillaging in the wee hours of the morning. Some of the fancier foods brought by visiting elders from other tribes tasted so delicious, my mouth watered in anticipation.

I removed my moccasins carefully from

my pained feet, taking caution to remove the moss padding I had put inside them earlier to soften the pain from the blistering and cold. They ached so bad from working fervently the past week, without a moments rest from sun up until sun down. Their stinging had become almost unbearable as I lowered them into the creek. I felt as if my heart would stop the moment they sank into the brisk, flowing water, and the tinges of pain crawled up my calves and into my knees. I closed my eyes, sighed a deep breath and wished I could scream. I closed my eyes and let my mind wander off to a happier place and time.

~

"ARRGH... NOOOO".... A high pitch cried out, vaulting like lightning through the evening air, almost sending me tumbling down the embankment and into the creek, it was so loud.

I must have fallen asleep, because I found myself disoriented. Stumbling as I jumped up in a panic, I squinted in the darkness to see if I could tell where the noise was coming from. Outside of the noises coming from the beginning of the celebration at the main camp echoing in the background, the air was still. I then heard rustling by the bridge crossing on the creek, and ducked down to hide, and try to see what was going on.

I saw shadows of people, but couldn't make out more than just images. I crept closer. Then, to my horror, I saw her.

My sister, Laylah was between two women and behind them, the Chief's son and they were heading across the bridge path.

She was sobbing. It pained me to see her that way. I felt an overwhelming cramping and nausea overtake me. I wanted so desperately to cry out to her, when all of a sudden I felt a hand on my shoulder.

I had been so consumed with watching what was taking place that I did not even notice my mother had come to stand next to me. I turned to her; tears began to stream down my face and I knew my biggest fear had come true. Although I had partially known it was inevitable one day, I had been in denial until now.

My mother choked back her tears, then wiped mine that had begun to flow quite heavily and motioned me towards out tipi, as she began to explain.

She said that word had come that there were no more eligible maidens in the main camp that were pleasing to Alisais, and the time had come when he must take a bride soon from somewhere and fulfill his destiny. He must start his own relations and prepare to take his rightful place as leader of the tribe since his father's health was failing. When he had come to the camp earlier, he had noticed my sister, whom he had been watching from a distance for some time and he was pleased with what he saw in her. He had chosen my sister as his bride and wanted her to be taken to the main camp and prepared. She was to be his wife.

Whether she wanted him as a husband or not," *it must be done for the good of our people*", my mother whispered as she held me close. "Come my daughter, we must get you inside you shaking terribly", momma said as she cradled my head against her shoulder as we entered our tipi.

I was so distraught I sank down onto my bedding of bison skin and elk, grasping it between my arms, knowing that my sister who had shared this same place of slumber with me for over a decade was now gone. Gone to be a bride, and I was left here, to be alone, among the *reclaimed.* I drifted off into a troubled sleep.

As I reached my hands under my headrest, I felt the bump in the earth below and remembered the beads we had hidden a while back, and cried even harder. Who would I share all my little secrets with? Now I had no one to confide in. I knew then that as soon as it was light again, I would take those beads and sew them onto my moccasins so I could look at them and remember the joy my sister and I had when we shared so many pleasurable memories and moments together. I cried myself to sleep, aching deep inside as it felt a part of me had died. I knew my sister deserved to take her rightful place among the pure-blood one day, but it still hurt deep inside to let her go.

~

My restless slumber was enhanced by the echoing sound of my mother snoring. Rubbing my eyes which had grown quite puffy and ached from crying, I reached over to feel the empty place in the bedding next to me, and felt the pain of emptiness take hold once again.

I wondered at that moment, would my sister be happy?

Would she miss me?

When would I see her again?

Is she ok?

I knew at that moment, while my mother was asleep and could not stop my foolish notion; I must sneak out to see for myself.

If not to get to talk to her, then I would have to settle for at least being able to catch a glimpse of her from behind the trees, in the distance. I crept quietly past my mother, being mindful not to wake her, and headed to sneak beyond the creek and over to the main camp.

The air had grown much colder than before. As I trampled through the brush along the creek and ducked under the bridge to sneak across quietly through the shallow part of the creek beneath, unseen, the coldness of the water soaked clear thru me. I pulled my face down into my shawl to hide the tell-tale breath in the cold night air that might be seen by someone as I drew closer to the bustling crowds of tribesmen and women gathering and feasting.

Chapter 5

Squinting and shivering, I made my way behind a tipi, and squatted down intending not to be seen. I searched the shadows of images gathered around the fire in a circle in hopes to catch an image of my sister somewhere among them.

If I could just see her face, her expression, I would hopefully be able to see if she were happy or frightened. I couldn't see her among any of the people outside, so I decided to lay low and listen, to hear if I could maybe locate where she might be.

Creeping along the outer edges of the tipis aligning the north end of the encampment. Listening and looking, while trying not to get caught, I began to hear soft voices coming from the tipi I had just ducked behind to avoid detection from people going in and out of it.

Catching my breath, and trying not to let my teeth chatter loudly. I doubted anyone would hear me in all the noise and bustle of everyone feasting and preparing for the dancing to come, so I sat on the ground and pulled my shawl up closer around my face to try and keep warm.

As I sat there in the night air, I thought I heard my sisters voice. Laylah had a soft high-pitched voice, unlike me, who my momma said sounded more like the voice of a youthful boy. Hers always radiated a kindness and compassion I recognized right away, as I heard her speaking to someone. She was right in the tipi I was hiding behind! Truly the Great Spirit had been kind in helping me find her so quickly!

I squatted down further and searched around the bottom of the outer caping of the bottom of the tipi, hoping to find some sort of small space or opening I might be able to squeeze a peek thru and catch a glimpse of my sister without being noticed. There were bundles of straw and dried cornstalks aligned along the bottom, which was customary to keep the cold drafts from seeping thru, and I pushed a few aside and crept down low, laying on my belly, pulling a few of the longer stalks over me to conceal my protruding body from sight. As I peered in, it was hard to see at first because my eyes had grown accustomed to the darkness outside and it took a bit of time to adjust to the light emanating from bound cloth torches. There were several hanging from mounts on staffs around the interior of what seemed to be one of the largest tipis I had ever seen.

As the spacious surroundings came into focus, I could see my sister sitting in one corner area, encircled by a few women who were placing strings of shells and bobbles around her neck, while one was painting markings upon her arms and another was braiding her hair, weaving small ribbons to and fro with each twist of her dark, silky locks.

She turned her head for a moment and I saw that she had a smile on her face. She looked absolutely radiant! I looked around the space and saw how beautiful the interior was decorated.

Right to the left of me I saw something similar to the sleeping things, they called *beds*, I saw in the white man's magazines. It had four corners made of tree trunks and ropes made from something I couldn't identify intertwined underneath and was piled nicely with blankets woven in fancy colors and an array of finely tanned skins. I was close enough, and the drums were starting to pick up a more audible rhythm, that I decided I would slowly creep in and under it, since it was high enough off the ground I could take refuge under it and see my sister as well as find a little relief from the cold that was making me shiver violently.

I was pleased with my stealth abilities as I drew my last foot in under the edging of the tipi, and laid quietly under the quite large object, watching as women came to and fro the entrance, each carrying some new item to either adorn my sister with or place on a table near her.

Confused, and yet mesmerized by all the fussing over Laylah, as I lay there peeking out from my hiding place, an itch welled up in my nose. I had been so preoccupied with the happenings going on before my eyes, I had not noticed I was inhaling dirt from off the flooring of the tipi.

Without warning, and no way to stop it, I let out a fierce sneeze that not only rang out like a bear angrily growling, but caused a hush to take hold in the tipi. It fell silent. As everyone began to peer down towards where I was hiding and pointing, I scampered backwards as fast as I could to try and retreat before they caught me.

I was startled near clean out of my buckskins as I backed up and prepared to get to my knees and flee, when I felt a tight grasp around both my ankles yank me flat and face first into the ground. Whomever it was proceeded to yank me the rest of the way out of the hay and begin to drag me across the ground like a fresh kill about to be taken and skinned on a rocky ledge.

Frightened to near insanity, I began to cry and ramble like a toddler caught stealing crumbs when I should be sleeping. I was drug halfway around the side of the tipi, when I heard a voice order them to stop, and I was forcefully rolled over, then spat upon by some woman, who then cursed and said, "it is that half-breed bitch". Angered and thinking to myself, how dare she, I am not a dog. I began to try and sit up and attempt to run away, defiantly, and failed.

I continued to sob, as I was being restrained by another older woman of such build and stature, which if not for the lack of fur, would have made me feel as if I had been captured by a grizzly bear. "It is the half-blood sister for sure" she shouted out loud and confirmed the first woman's comments.

I cried out sobbingly;

"I want to see her".

"I want to   see my sister and say good-bye".

Then held my head down in shame for my foolishness, hoping I had not brought on any future turmoil for Laylah.

I was covered in dirt and tears with hair disheveled when   I heard heavier footsteps coming towards me. As the feet drew close and stopped in front of me, I recognized the moccasins from seeing them on Alisais as he came through our camp earlier that day. Had he come around the end of the tipi to see what all the commotion was about and have me punished or even banished?

When they told him who I was, I hung my head even lower in shame, hoping he wouldn't see my tear stained muddy face and send me away. He didn't. Instead he told the women I was to be allowed to see my sister, and held out his hand to help me to my feet. He instructed them to clean the dirt from off my face and let me be with my sister. He walked away waving his hand in the air in a gesture of exasperation as he said to the women, *"just a few minutes to say farewell and then drag her off; such filth juvenile of white man!*

I was then led towards the front of the tipi and into the opening to where my sister was still being prepared for the ceremony to come. I was so excited that I would get a few moments to see Laylah that I didn't care what that evil man who stole my sister from me thought. Nor did I care about the vile comments made by the woman who spat at me. I wanted to see Laylah, and tell her I loved her.

I sat there knelt at her feet, as she beckoned for someone to get a cloth to clean the smudges on my face. I had not noticed the scratches I had received while being drug across the ground until she was gently cleaning the dirt away from my cheeks and smiling at me. I was holding her other hand tightly as she reassured me she was happy to be chosen to be the bride and first wife of Alisais, who would one day be a powerful chief and the leader of our tribal nation.

I was comforted in her words as she promised that she would do everything she could to assure that I saw her often. I felt a sense of warmth and peace overcome me when she spoke gently and said that this was what the Great Spirit wanted, and that no matter what happened in the future, she would love me forever. My heart was at ease.

~

I cried as she held me close and she stroked my hair, picking out some of the straw that had gotten tangled in it when I was slithering about under the edges of the tipi.

Visions of her and I sitting together as children playing and our shared warm moments ran through my mind that moment. She always had a way of bringing me peace and comfort when I felt troubled. Her reassuring word that I would always be her sister, and in her heart brought me some comfort.

Our time was cut short when that smelly, grizzly-bear of a woman returned with a scornful look on her face. I am sure it was because of her obvious disapproval of half-bloods among the pure-blood when she blurted out;

"you may watch from a distance and keep your mouth shut"!

I was excited yet saddened at the same time as I was forcefully taken out of the tipi and told to sit on a prickly pile of hay a distance away from all the others. I was just close enough to see the fire and hear the sounds, but barely able to catch the glimpse of my sisters face as she was escorted to her rightful place next to her soon-to-be husband.

Alisais sat there in full ceremonial feathers and dress holding her hand. She looked so beautiful! She was about to be married to the second-most powerful man in our tribe who actually looked quite handsome next to her. My subconscious wanted to smack me for that momentary thought.

How could I even remotely think him handsome after he had stolen her from me!

Perhaps it was because I saw how happy she was standing next to him. Either way, my mind was confused and between being pleased she was happy, and the longing I knew I would feel when I would be back at our camp once again and not have her around to spend my days with.

The music and dancing paused the moment Chief Stumblingbear rose to his feet and summoned his son and Laylah to proceed forward from where they were waiting and he began their ceremonial joining chants and prayers.

As he continued with blessings and chants, his body grew weary and his deep voice began trembling, showing his age and rapidly declining poor health.

My sister glowed in the illumination from the fire. I could see the glistening in her eyes and the pleasant smile on her face. I was pleased that this union was what she seemed to truly want. I couldn't have been happier to see her at peace with it despite the emptiness I felt in the pit of my stomach, knowing the changes this would make in our future closeness.

Chapter 6

Nearly a whole year had passed. Another long hot summer that lasted far into the fall season had finally drawn to a close. I was almost ecstatic to welcome the winter months, despite how brutally cold they would soon become. So many changes took place this past summer and I had finally come to terms with my sister not being around.

Accepting her happiness the night she was joined with Alisais and the overwhelming look of pleasure in her eyes, was enough to bring me comfort on the long days I worked alone. I had begun to move on and accepted life as it would now be.

Day in and day out I worked and enjoyed the warmth of the sun, and was pleased that over the past year my skin had begun to darken and I was looking quite a bit less like a half-blood and more like I actually belonged among our people. I had started my journey to womanhood and had wondered why so many found it an exciting journey. How could having cramping pain and bleeding a joy?

Momma told me sometimes growing up we change, and she was right in far more ways that I dare mention. I was not sure why, but my daytime lollygagging and dreaming of wanting things in the white man's books had started to diminish over time and I started picturing what it would be like to have a warrior for myself one day. Not that it would likely happen, but I had heard from eavesdropping on some of the conversations in the main camp, that many of the other tribes nearby never treated half-bloods as cruelly as our tribe did, and wondered would I be looked at equally one day too?

~

Gossip was one thing that could always be heard as women washed clothing, bathed or gathered water along the banks of the creek, or whisper among themselves like cackling hens as they were gathered around in circles chaffing wheat or stripping corn from cobs to dry for later use.

The latest gossip being muttered among the older womenfolk was that my sister was with child. It seemed any time they saw me coming nearby they would hush themselves or change the topic of conversation. So I did my best to sneak around and listen where I would not be noticed as much. I would just come right out and ask my sister, but it was rare I was allowed anywhere near her, and the few times I did get close enough it was so brief, we could only so much as smile at one another and move on. It did irritate me that I had to hear it through the usual gossip grapevine that she was with child and not from my sister herself.

The Chief was also looking towards having his son step in and take over, as his health was declining. I didn't care about the Chief really, I had a disdain for him ever since I learned how much he hated any half-blood since his sister was killed by one many years ago. He treated us like it was our fault she was taken. I was however excited for my sister if the rumor was true and she was going to have a baby.

Each time there were whispers and gossip, I made it a point to try and get as close to the chatter to hear of any news I could. I did not get to see my sister close up lately. As the winter months set in, it seemed she was rarely outside of her tipi. The few times I did get a glimpse of her, it was hard for me to tell if she looked with child because she was always bundled from the cold with bulky fur clothing and wraps.

The latest rumor for the week was that Alisais would be seeking help from one of the girls in the camp or from a neighboring tribes village as a servant and hand maiden to Laylah instead of taking on the traditional second wife, as our custom usually dictated. Yes, it was true that usually a younger sister of a bride would be chosen to fill that obligation or role, but I knew that was far-fetched and unlikely considering the circumstances.

Alisais, just like his father, the Chief, had showed in the past, a firm dislike for half-breeds. I do recall him referring to me as *filthy*. I knew tradition would most likely be broken since the second wife was usually picked from the sisters of his current wife and I was unacceptable by the tribes standards, I knew that this customary practice was not an option he would be seeking.

Alisais had made it plain and clear the night he married my sister, what he thought of me. I suppose that he only allowed me to say my good-byes and watch Laylah marry him so she would not fight or possibly resist his intentions with her. Or would he be different? What would his choices have been if his overbearing father weren't still ruling the camp?

If my sister were with child, I did want to be by her side. Part of me feared for Laylah and her well-being since I had heard so many horror stories from my crazy aunt and others just how awful bearing a child on the prairie could be. The mortality rate among our people was changing with the onset of some of the white man's diseases that had spread during trading with them and their passing thru our areas. I wished I could be with her. Half-blood or not, I should be helping care for her, not some stranger, an outsider, but family!

~

Childbirth was something never really talked about among our people. I remember as a young girl, asking my mother about having children. Either she would totally ignore me, or she would say *"if one day you are even chosen as a bride out of desperation, you will learn when the time comes to give birth"*. Being I was now almost 15, I knew enough from idle chatter and observation all the rituals and happenings that being pregnant and child bearing entailed.

When a woman first learns of her pregnancy she is by order of her husband to cease doing many of the things she normally would do, to guarantee a safe pregnancy and continue the growth of the tribe.

There were the legends and superstitions passed down from one generation to another, said to be messages of warning from the Great Spirit, that must be adhered to in order for a child to be born healthy. This led to many rituals and practices based on the legendary superstitions that that had to be respected as well.

For instance, pregnant women are banned from eating the heart and innards of animals normally one consumes for fear it will darken her facial complexion and she might start to resemble the black slaves the white man owns. If she eats leg muscles of any cloven hoof animal, she is bound to have leg cramps the whole time she is pregnant, and if she eats brains, she will bear a child who has a snotty nose and bad manners.

Pregnant women could not stand in the doorway of their tipi or lodge to gaze out. If there was anything she wanted to see outside, she must exit all the way out and stand away from the doorway. If she didn't go out far enough away from the door, superstition was that her labor would be very long and hard and the baby might not emerge alive from the womb.

With all these restrictions, surely Alisais would be looking for someone to help keep his household, and competently care for Laylah when the time came. Surely he loved her enough to provide the best for her considering she one day would be the wife of a Chief.

What if no one was available, then he would be forced to choose from some pure-blood orphan staying in our end of the camp?

It is rare but happens that such a maiden is chosen as a helper, but would be forced to keep her face adorned in a scarf or masking at all times and not look upon the man of the household or his wife for fear of bringing a curse or shame upon them. I had heard of other camps doing this, but many of those camps were less brutal to their own, even half-bloods were treated better than we were.

As I sat next to the fire with my mother, I

listened silently as she spoke to my aunt about the Chief's health declining, the latest gossip among the women of the main camp and Alisais' desire to make changes to some of the tribe's traditions once he was in command. I began to think that perhaps there would be hope in my future. Perhaps one day I could be considered an equal among the people.

Our population had dwindled over the years and Alisais had expressed among the other elders his fear that we might not survive much longer if care wasn't taken to be more accepting like other tribes as well as being more cautions to provide good care and help for all the women in the camp who were eligible to bear the future generations. I also wondered just how much that ideology made his father's skin crawl, and would chuckle to myself. If anyone deserved to have his skin itch and be irritated, it was Chief Stumblingbear, who I think should have been named Chief Grizzly-full-of-meanness-bear instead!

My mother, despite being sent to the reclaimed camp, was looked upon as a smart woman by many. Her brother, the Chief, although never acknowledging their being siblings in ceremonial fashion, did have several of the prided women of the camp seek out her advice. I was once told that she lost her place as an elder in the main camp when it was learned I was a half-blood and he shamed her for something that wasn't even her fault. I hated the man for this!

My momma told my aunt Mayma that as the eldest female of the reclaimed camp, she was given the task of choosing a pure-blood to be sent up to the main camp to be maiden help for my sister If there was no one mature enough then she was to set out with a few warriors to look among some of the smaller outlying camps for help. "It must be done quickly and with discretion", she relayed to my aunt.

I listened a little longer as I struggled to fight the exhaustion from my long day, and as the words drifted to my ears as they chatted, I was unsure if I were dreaming or was what I was hearing real? Discretion was far from their thoughts as my mother continued speaking, and relaying that she had a different plan in mind!

She then held her finger to her lips as if to say "hush, and as I rolled over on my bedding to drift off in a well needed slumber, I heard small rumbles   as they talked way into the night.   I was too tired to care what their conversation was about. I was ready to dream of my future and one day marrying a great warrior of my own.   No matter what our tribes customs were, my dreams were mine. My escape into a world of hope and possibilities of love and happiness would be found as I drifted off.

I knew if there was anything important that involved me, I would know about it in the morning. One could never tell what was being schemed so secretly between my mother and my aunt, who everyone thought was a lunatic.

Little did I know their scheming that night and their decisions would change my world forever.

Chapter 7

Wrapping an extra layer of cloth and skins around me after waking from a restless sleep, I greeted the new day's tasks of milking goats and gathering wood for the camps. Although still tired, I was feeling very cheery and warm inside. Not sure why, but today, for some reason, I felt was going to be a wonderful day.

Father sky had blessed us with a small round of snow that dusted the landscape overnight. It was always beautiful to see the first snowfall and how it shimmered and glistened on the waning foliage and ground in the sunrise, as if to give greetings to Mother Earth and welcome the new day.

I finished milking the goats and collecting eggs from the chickens that seemed to always lay their eggs in the strangest of places and hunting them is even more an adventure if they happened to have laid them and abandoned their nests to take cover from the snow right afterwards. They did not seem to be as smart as the other foul in the wild, which had more sense than to lay their eggs in the open for varmints to snatch. I took them back to our encampment where they would be sorted and put into baskets with other things such as dried berries and nuts I would carry up to the main camp later in the day.

Why on earth we even bothered caring for these pesky little feathered birds that chased and pecked at our feet and legs was beyond any rationale I could muster, but they were a gift from one of the families of another tribe out east, in a place called Illinois. They had been given to his tribe as part of some trade pact with the white man. They may have tasted good cooked in the many ways we had cooked eggs from the wild foul in the area, but as mean as they would get at times, I would have much rather seen them plucked and strung for buzzards to pick at instead.

I heard it was some man named Taft, Chief of the white people, who had given us these chickens along with many other new items we were experiencing, such as coffee, and this new sweet thing they called taffy. The taffy tasted so good, but would stick to my teeth and feel like every time I tried to chew, I would surely pull one of my molars clean out of its socket!

I started paying more attention to the talking's at the main camp when I could. I suppose it was because I had matured quite a bit over the summer, that I wanted to know more about the adult things that went on around camp and the rest of this America I had never seen any of.

Rumor was, this Taft man had great ideas on trading and commerce between white men and us natives and hoped for peace. I was not sure if this was true or was it another trap to force more people from the plains to the reservations as had been done so many times past.

This Taft man made another Chief like person named Valentine take charge in the reformations. He was tasked with "finding a way to make the white man rule our lands and keep all natives and savages under control", is how the Chief put it. For once, I was inclined to agree with that grizzly aging man I despised.

Just let them near me I thought to myself.

I will show them savage alright!

Over the last few months we had seen many new trinkets some of the white men had traded for our furs and seeds we gathered. They were wonderful to look at, yet I, like many others, still hated them but pretended to be friendly just so the white man wouldn't use that loud rifle thing to eliminate us. Some of us were frightened they would shoot us dead with the lead bullets that seemed to magically travel out of the rifles faster than a jackrabbit running from a fox.

~

Enough of my nonsense thinking and wasting time, I had work to do. Humming to myself as I gathered sticks for kindling, I saw my Aunt waving her arms frantically at me to get my attention. She was beckoning for me to come up to the tipi mid morning, which was rare that she was even outside this early in the day, so I knew it must be important. I approached her with curiosity and a quizzical expression as I started to speak and inquire what was so important that she be flailing her arms as if they were on fire to draw my attention. She motioned for me to be silent, and pulled me by my arm when I reached her, pulling me into the tipi.

Suspiciously she peeked outside one last time, looking from side to side, which started to alarm me. She was looking from side to side as if she had just done something horrible and was in fear that someone may have noticed the quick retreat into the tipi. No sooner than she had poked her head back inside and she motioned towards a stool in the corner.

"Hurry and sit down, we have little time". "Your momma and I have a plan, and I must prepare you as much as I can with the details, before she gets back and it will be time to put things in motion", she said nervously. I complied, with a perplexing look on my face. I had never seen my aunt act this frantic, and believe me, sometimes she did some really bizarre stuff and this bordered frightening!

I sat there confused, as she explained the scheme mom and her had come up with. I thought to myself,

"Mayma you have completely lost your mind for sure, and taken my momma with you!"

Momma and Mayma had hatched a plan to not tell the rest of our camp about the request for a helper for the new young chief and my sister.

They would send me instead!

My momma arrived back at the tipi shortly after Mayma had explained the crazy plan. She continued explaining in greater detail where Aunt Mayma left off.

I definitely began to think they were both going totally insane!

She said, "Since you're not to speak much, and must always keep your head covered outside of the tipi and face away from the chief and his relations as not to look upon them, no one will know it is you". I did love the idea of being with my sister at this most important time in her life, but was also mortified that if they found out I would surely be killed for my deceit. Desperate to be a part of my sister's life again, despite the risks, I knew I would do anything to be there for Laylah no matter what!. I agreed to go along with their crazy scheme and actually started to feel just as excited as I was frightened of the consequences.

Over the next few hours my momma, aunt and I began taking steps to put the scheme into motion. It was a good thing I had been very mindful of some of the other tribes women who had maidens and how their interactions were over the last several months, because it made it easier to understand what would be expected of me. I would make every effort to keep my face covered at all times, so no one, even from our camp, would notice that it was me, a half-blood even though I had darkened up as I aged to almost be as darkly complexioned as the rest of our tribe. I could do nothing to hide my blue eyes though, a dead give-away, something was different!

Avoiding eye contact would be easy if I stayed very dedicated to my sister and her husband's household needs, so no one would call into question my loyalties and confront me. Even if it meant I was to lower myself to groveling at their feet, I would. I just knew I could do this.

I would make sure I was never caught bathing where anyone who could recognize me among other workers and report me to the elder's to win favors in the eyes of those in power. I had to be very cautious so not to expose the deceit. Inside I trembled in utter fear of my demise should I be found out, but being with my sister again was worth the price I might pay later.

My mother dressed me in one of her nice

dresses she had stored away, then had me put on a pair of her nice beaded moccasins my grandfather had given her nearly 20 years ago on her wedding day. I had remembered seeing the colorful and intricately beaded moccasins and putting them on, made me feel proud and beautiful inside and out. I covered my head with a scarf and looked at my mother and Mayma, and tried not to cry. I knew I would miss them dearly, but this was my chance for change as well. As my mother leaned forward to wipe a tear that had fallen from my eyes she kissed my cheek and hugged me. Excited and frightened, I knew this was good-bye.

She then told me that I was to meet some women on the foot path on the other side of the bridge, at sunset. The elders had been busy with meetings among Chiefs from several tribes and there would be no warrior escort to come collect the hand-maiden chosen.

We reviewed all the plans and the ways I would try to keep my identity undisclosed and my mamma told me all the of things that are usually expected of women in situations of pregnancy and helping. She tried as best she could to fit in to the brief amount of time we had left. When I inquired as to what she would tell the other people in our camp of the reclaimed, she merely stated that she would tell them I had been snatched by some white folk and hauled off to a missionary settlement. It is not likely anyone from the main camp would question my disappearance, as long as their needs were being met by us workers.

I just hoped the idea would work, and maybe I would be good enough at the tasks expected of me, that one day I might be lucky enough to be worthy of a husband and children. A girl could dream couldn't she?

She hugged me one last time and turned away to hide her tears as she whispered, "you had better hurry since time was fast approaching".

As I headed out into the cold evening air, I looked over my shoulder to see her and my aunt, both in tears waving me on. Frightened as a wild boar staring down as a hunter's arrow plunges deep into its side, I trembled waiting for them on the path that snowy evening. I was shivering violently and I was not sure if it was the cold, or the fright that made me tremble so. I began to think even the wildlife could hear my teeth chattering in the night air, as I awaited my future.

Not soon after I arrived in the designated waiting spot, I was greeted by two plump ladies who seemed very rushed and bothered that they had to come retrieve me, and quickly escorted me to the main camp, all the while, complaining that they hoped I was well disciplined enough to do my job, because with all the new trading with the white men and their fancy for our hand-crafted bead items, no one had time to "babysit and train" an idiot.

I was quite offended, and wanted to blurt a rude retort, but held my tongue. I wanted to at least not anger anyone any time soon. I just wanted to see my sister and do my job. I simply replied, "I have been trained well and will do as asked, to be pleasing to the family of the dwelling for which I am tasked". They seemed satisfied with that answer and we walked the rest of the short distance in silence.

Chapter 8

I was escorted to the tipi of my sister and her husband Alisais. I was quickly instructed by his mother, who was waiting there for my arrival, as to where I would be sleeping and what was to be expected of me. Then she hastily retreated and left me to be alone with Laylah. Laylah asked me to help her ready up the household for the evening meditation so she could rest because she was exhausted.

I smiled and proceeded to start tidying things up, content that she had not looked directly at me nor asked my name. In all the quick planning and focus on detail my momma and aunt had done the hours prior, the one thing they had forgotten to mention, was my name. In a brief moment of worry, I had to think of one, and fast.

I froze right where I stood, sure enough as Laylah approached me, inquiring as to my name. Panic set in and I felt as if a buffalo had just trampled the very breath out of me.

This is my sister.

How could I lie to her?

Would she accept me, or would she shun me and uphold the rules of the tribe and cast me into the hands of the elders to have me punished for my deceit?

Wetness began to well in my eyes as a lump formed in my throat as I gasped and softly replied submissively;

"My name does not matter; you may call me as you choose".

I turned my head away, as tears began to stream down my face. I wanted to reach out and wrap my arms around her and feel the kindness I grew up knowing in my sister's embrace. I hoped for the same acceptance I had always felt over our many youthful years passed, but I was just as frightened of how time may have changed her.

That instant, as I stood cemented in place, unable to move from utter fright, I felt her moving closer towards me. She grabbed me by my arm and snatched the scarf off my head. She looked at me with amazement, wiped my tear stained cheeks with her sleeve and smiled.

That moment, as I looked in her eyes, I

knew that the bonds of sisterhood did mean more to her than any tribal rules or traditions.

I was her sister, and she loved me!

We embraced one another and spent a few moments in tears, then we sat together on a makeshift fur laden bench by the fire sharing stories and catching up on the latest rumors and gossip in the camp. I learned that most of the tales I had heard were true. We were doing more trading with the white men and more tribes were coming together to make sure that our people were no longer harmed by the white man, nor tricked by some of the "missionaries" that passed thru in hopes to reform our savage ways by claiming to offer a better life elsewhere.

She spoke of the kindness of her husband and the many things he one day hoped to change once he was the Chief, and after his father passed. She explained that any of his ideas offered now, his dad shunned because it was not the ways of the past. She told me that secretly she hated him as much as I did and that was a relief.

We also decided I needed a name and we quickly agreed on calling me *Wakinyela*, because she said I had the grace of a swan to have been able to gracefully sneak right into the main camp and into her tipi without anyone noticing that I was not brought up in the more *refined* dwellings in the tribe. I filled her in on how it came about, and she chuckled at the ingenuity of my mother and aunt to devise such a scheme since moms health was so frail and my aunt was just plain nuts most of the time.

She explained that if we were careful, we could pull this plot of deceit my mother had started. She would help me any way she could. But should I get caught, she would have no choice but to deny any knowledge of the deceit and I would have to accept my punishment alone. I understood that. Knowing the Chief was still alive, he would not be as gracious as I am sure Alisais would be, since my sister spoke of his secret wishes for change so heartily.

She made me promise to never let anyone catch a glimpse of me without a head covering when outside of the tipi or when the tipi was well lit and they had guests. She explained that Alisais had been so busy learning the ways of the tribe and his new responsibilities soon to come, he was rarely ever in her presence until darkness had fallen, and he probably wouldn't notice.

She explained that she would have to pretend she did not know me prior to me arriving in her tipi, and she must treat me as a servant so as not to draw suspicion when he or other outsiders were around. I understood and loved her so much, I did not care. I was there, with her, we were together and I would do anything, everything I could to never allow us to be separated again.

Laylah began to speak more about her husband. She said that she was happy to be married to Alisais, whom she grew to love very much. She said that he was very kind and gentle to her. She spoke of all the changes to the tribe he hoped for when it was his time to take over as Chief when his father passed on to the Great Spirit Land. She spoke with such compassion, I knew she truly loved him and he loved her.

Just six more moons before her baby would come into the world, and she was so excited to be preparing for the start of her growing relations and motherhood. She also shared with me her worries as to how she was feeling lately. She had become so exhausted at simply getting out of bed on some mornings, that she feared any overworking would cause her to lose their child. So many children had succumb to their fate before even having a chance to take their first breath or live longer than a few moons after birth due to the rampant spread of this thing she called *smallpox*. It was a disease that managed to come along as fast as the white man who carried it. She wanted everything to go well.

We had so much to catch up on during the many private moments we would have alone and even much more to get ready for with the arrival of her child.

This would be the first child to be born in almost five years among the people. Everyone in the camp was excited. Every precaution would have to be taken to make sure Laylah remained well rested and looked after. Alisais and his father were determined to see to that!

The first few days seemed the hardest, as I battled to remain distant and more as a servant than a sibling to Laylah. But I was able to settle in to a routine quite quickly. Good thing it was a brutal winter, and everyone covered up heavily to protect themselves from the elements, so it was not hard for me to disguise who I was under many layers of warmth, when duties require I leave the tipi briefly. For once, I was thankful to the Great Spirit for imposing such blustery conditions upon our community for once.

When Alisais was around the dwelling, he was always doting on my sister and I was happy to see how much he truly did care for her. Even happier because that meant he was paying no attention to me, to notice who I really was, despite having done much maturing over the last year since he saw me, and resembling very little of the youthful and defiant girl he spoke so harshly to the night he married my sister.

JENAI DAWN

Chapter 9

Days turned into weeks. I gathered wood, fetched ice to melt from the frozen creek for water, cooked, cleaned and milked the goat tied up in a shanty right out behind the tipi to make sure that everything was perfect and milk for strength was fresh and abundant for my sister and Alisais.

As I spent more and more time in the company of my sister and her husband, helping them as best I could. It seemed to please Alisais that someone could be so dedicated to his wife and her needs. He complemented me a few times and I am glad he didn't see me blush or recognize me.

It pleased him well enough that I once overheard him talking to his mother one evening when she came to visit, bringing with her, fresh fry-bread and dried fruits, and exclaiming that how nice it would be if he could find such a handy person for him to take as his second wife one day, that was as caring as I was to the needs of his tipi. I had grown fond of Alisais and cherished the notion that perhaps one day it could be me, but knew that was a fantasy.

It was part of her nature to frequently scold him for not taking on another wife before the arrival of his child. Someone had to care for him and his personal needs as well as the household when his wife was in her time of confinement and after childbirth.

As she spoke those words she headed over to me, and leaned in try and uncover my face and get a glimpse to see if I was even worthy of her son. Only the best in beauty would do. I felt like I wanted to just vomit at her suggestion of butting in where she didn't belong.

My sister immediately protested the chilliness in the air and asked me to help her to her warm bedding that lay in the darkness of the corner and out of her mother-in-laws prying eyes.

What a speedy diversion and I had to love my sisters ingenuity and swiftness!!

I would have surely fainted right there had she not been so quick to intervene. I had to make sure from then on that I never came close enough to that nosey and prudish woman who was bound and determined to have her son, the future leader of our tribe, have as many wives as possible to bring as many children into the relations as he could.

It was true our tribe had been rapidly decreasing with the spread of the many white man's diseases brought into the camps, but this woman had radical ideals I wanted no part of.

She, as well as the chief were so dead set in expanding, they acted as if they should line women up on all fours and let him spread his seed like the wolves during the spring mating season! I would have none of that, unless...

Could he ever find me as loveable as he did my sister?

True, he was quite the warrior. With the finest of appearance as if to be the grandest of buffet to the hungry soul, I still would dare not partake of the kneeling on all fours, to any man, unless he loved me for more than just my ovaries and offspring. Yet secretly in my heart, I felt a bit of an attraction to him.

What had brought on these strange feelings of late?

What had begun to draw me to this man, why was I starting to like a man who spewed such vile hatred towards me just a year ago?

Was it because he made my sister happy?

Or was I starting to see more of who he really was when he was away from the other men in the tribe?

Alisais, when alone with my sister in their tipi, was not the harsh soon-to-be leader he appeared to be when standing among the elders and his father who was always demanding perfection. He was a warm and gentle soul.

Always showing so much kindness and warmth, embodied with love and compassion whenever he spent time with her, I found myself jealous and longing to one day have such a man to treat me the same.

Could I secretly be falling in love with him too?

I knew this was only a dream for me, a fantasy that I would live out, only if it were just in my mind. Who among our people would give of themselves this kind of love to a half-blood so unworthy? Besides, Alisais' mother was just as overbearing with tradition and old values as his father, and if she even knew that a half breed were anywhere nearby her or in the home of her son, she would surely have them taken out and stoned. I needed to give up such thoughts of nonsense and focus only on the tasks ahead.

Months passed, soon the baby would arrive, and my sister was becoming more pained and unable to move. Alisais called for the medicine man to come visit. Afraid she would succumb to the many tribulations our women had bearing children among the plains lately, one must seek out chants inspired by the Spirit and herbs from the medicine man, to rid them of any evil that may wish to whisk away the very life of our future.

Seeing the concern in Alisais' eyes, as he sat by her side waiting for help to arrive, I could feel his emotion and see his love and devotion to her. I knew then that I *had* started to fall in love with this kind and gentle man.

The medicine man had arrived and I made my way to the far side of the tipi to hide in the shadows. I knew for sure he would recognize me from the many times he was called to look in on my mother who had taken ill many times over the past several months.

He administered teas and there was chanting late into the night as he said blessings and prayers for her healing and I continued to prepare the night meal for Alisais and keep water hot and ready for the nasty potions of healing teas for Laylah. She seemed to be feeling much better, but needed her rest, so he instructed Laylah to rest, and do nothing more than eat and walk, until the arrival of her child due the next full moon to come.

He said it would be a spring baby most likely. But the baby could arrive one moon earlier than expected if she was not careful to heed his instruction. If she rested and followed his orders, the child would have a better chance of survival.

I knew more responsibility would fall on me, and was ready for the challenge that lay ahead. This was my sister, my best friend, and I would do anything for her.

Just as Alisais had settled in on the bedding next to my sister for the night, his mother came storming into the tipi demanding to speak to her son. He immediately rose and scornfully instructed her to meet him outside, because he wanted it to remain quiet for Laylah to get rest.

I could hear them talking argumentatively outside of the tipi for a few moments. She kept insisting that if he was not going to marry another wife, then he should at least find a few more chosen young women, to have available to at least lay with and impregnate to secure some guaranteed offspring should Laylah lose her life in childbearing. Alisais was outraged, and voiced it curtly as he proceeded to tell his mother to go away, and he returned into the warm tipi and rested once again next to my sister.

I quietly finished tidying up and headed to sleep as well, knowing that the next several days were going to be long and worrisome for all. I could not understand how anyone would be so driven by status in a tribe, based on offspring and appearances of success to think of such carnality without love involved. She was such a heartless individual. I had just a mind to tell her so one day! But knew for now I must just bite my tongue and do what was expected of me.

I lay there drifting off to sleep. Then there was that voice in my head that spoke to me, the one I always felt frightened of in the past, but had not heard in so long. I had remembered before momma telling me that it was always a gift to be spoken to by the Great Spirit, but I was more convinced because I was a half-blood that it might be the white man's demons coming to haunt me again, and restlessly battled the flooding words and thoughts they created in my head.

As I drifted in and out that night, I saw images of fire, a funeral and burning of cleansing incense that woke me in a sweat of panic and fear. As I lay there silently, hoping that the crying out I made, was only in my dream as well, and as I glanced at my sister and Alisais sleeping peacefully, I knew it was.

I laid my head back down and prayed for the Spirit to please give me strength and peace and help my sister to get better, and the courage to stay civil and not choke Alisas' mother the next time I saw her. Although seeing her trampled by a herd of late migrating buffalo to hilly shelter one winter afternoon while she was out and about would be a pleasant view to see. I smiled as I pictured that happening to such an evil, meddling woman as I drifted back to sleep.

JENAI DAWN

Chapter 10

The days seemed to go on forever. Not only was there more working sunlight as spring approached, but the mounting tasks and expectations imposed by my sister's mother-in-law, for her son's household, grew immense. It was enough to care for my sister, without her adding on so many tasks irrelevant to her care and more focused on "appearances". I was at my wits end and exhausted! Some days I felt as if she only came around and demanded things of me as a means of torture for her miserable existence, knowing I would dare never argue with her demands. It wasn't that I was passive and didn't care that she treated me like a dog, I just didn't want her to ever confront me and discover my true identity.

Oh how nice it would be for a giant eagle to swoop down from the sky and pluck the wretched woman from off the plains and drop her in the sea so far away,

I thought to myself quite often.

In the evenings when my sister had eaten her meager evening meal and retired to bed, I would sit by my bedding and work on some of the clothing I was making for her babies arrival. It was in those late evening moments I began to notice her husband off in the distance, watching me when he thought I was not looking. The way he looked, as his barren chest and that sleek muscular body seemed to glow radiantly in the dim light of the fire. The image sent butterflies straight down to the very core of my stomach.

Why was he looking at me?

Was I doing something wrong or displeasing to him?

Or was it something else?

And....

why the hell did it give me this feeling of uneasiness in my belly?

Whenever I saw him noticing I was looking back, I hurried to hide my eyes and move as far out of view as I could. This of course in a tipi is almost utterly impossible to do.

I learned how little privacy there really was the very first week I arrived in my sister's household. Especially when they had their alone time, and my only means of escape, was burying my head completely under my bedding skins, sticking my fingers in my ears and pretending I couldn't hear a thing or wandering off to nap a few hours with the goat in the shanty out back, just to get some well needed rest in silence.

I have to admit, I did peek out a few times from

under the covers of sheer curiosity, considering what a married couple does after dark was unknown to me outside of my rumor-ridden education by babbling women doing chores and spreading tales. My precocious nature always drove me to the point I had to seek answers to even the oddest of questions in my head., making a point to ignore other peoples renditions and learning for myself what reality was.

Many a time, the interaction between my sister and Alisais was so gentle and loving, I found myself laying there in the still of the night imagining it were me, and some great warrior as my mate. Or even him. Boy was I starting to lose my mind or what? No way he or any other good warrior would ever think to take a second glance at this half-blood. But I still longed for it. I longed for a man, with whom I could love and would love me, would make me feel complete. If he had even half the good looks and build as Alisais, I know I would surely have been pleased.

Some nights as I lay there dreaming while awake, I would have overwhelming urges to be caressed and loved. Feeling the warm sensations these thoughts led to, I would catch myself craving the feeling of that touch and warmth, even if it required using my imagination and my own hand. My longing for experiencing this satisfaction and pleasure I heard my sister often express when Alisais loved and made love to her would draw me to seek my own happy place.

As the wanton urge grew stronger I would find my hand sliding down my thigh to the most warm an intimate part of my body all the while picturing it being a man who loved me, touching me. Envisioning how wonderful if someday, one day, someone would caress me there, love me, make love to me, and I would succumb to the vision of tenderness and then my release, quietly... alone.

~

The night was a very blustery one. We had heard the wise council advisor speak of heavy storms to come as prophesied in the clouds for two days, and now it seems that very storm was upon us. Winds were ripping at the sides of the tipi as if the skins used to cover its frame were going to be ripped clear from their bindings. Great effort was taken to secure the tipis earlier in the day by the men and extra straw was laid along the bottoms of the exterior wall in attempts to keep the brutal cold out and the heat of the fires in.

Extra bundles of wood had been collected and piled closer to each tipi and everyone drew to their beds after an early supper in hopes to rest under bedding and sleep through the harshest of the winds to pass overnight.

The cold dampness crept close to where I was resting, and although the fire was amply producing flames and warmth, I was far enough away that it did little to take away the chill that seemed to invade clean thru my skin, right to the bone in the bed where I lay alone, with no one to share body heat with.

I began to hear my sister mutter in her sleepy whispered voice and I sat up to look over to check on her. I knew she was starting to feel better lately despite the weather outside, and did not want her to get chilled and take a turn for the worse again. As my eyes began to gain focus in the darkness, I noticed she was alone.

I decided to get up and check on her, assuming that Alisais had gone over to smoke and drink while talking with father. He did this often after Laylah fell asleep for the night. I wanted to make sure that she was warm and comfortable so I got out from under my covers, and donned my moccasins and wrap and headed over to where she was.

I must have failed to pay close enough attention to my surroundings and been so focused on my sister, that I didn't see Alisais as he reentered the tipi because I ran straight into him with a bundle of extra furs I had grabbed from off a pile nearby. I didn't dare look up. Surely he was looking after my sister and the warmth of the tipi to be bringing in extra wood this late in the night. I froze in my tracks, not sure what to say, other than "I am sorry", as the words crackled from between my lips that were chapped and trembling, fearing reprimand for my clumsiness. He immediately turned away and dropped the sticks by the side of the fire and approached me.

Then I felt his hands gently glide under mine, to remove the blankets from my arms, as he said to me, "Let me take those, you have worked far too long today and need rest." He then explained that Laylah was resting well and just dreaming. He would make sure she was warm and he would tend to her and that I needed to not neglect getting rest of my own.

I retreated back to my resting place but could not find the comfort to fall asleep. Running through my mind, as if a herd of wild mustangs upon the range, were images of the moments preceding. The simple gesture of kindness had an overwhelming affect on me.

His touch, that feel, I could not erase from my thoughts.

The moment Alisais slid his hands across mine, the electrifying feel of his smoothness, his warmth the tenderness sank so deep in the lustful depths of my inner goddess. I was in love!

How could I betray my sister like this?

But how could I stop the growing emotions I was feeling?

How could I have such selfish thoughts about my sister's husband as she lay ill awaiting the arrival of their child?

I felt shameful, yet alive with desire. I admonished myself silently but became so overcome with lust and wanton that I could feel the moistness of my excitement building up, and could do nothing to ease the ache I felt.

As I turned away from the view of the fire and Alisais in the distance, I told myself that I must forego these notions and talk to my sister tomorrow and ask to be replaced. I couldn't allow myself to feel this way.

I knew that even if she had to create a story, in order to admonish me and have me banished from her tipi, something had to be done. I really did not want to leave her in her time of need and the baby so soon to come but I had to get out of there if I could not control my feelings and emotions towards Alisais.

He was my sister's husband, our tribe's future leader, and I wanted him! I know that many Elders and Chiefs had more than one wife, that they loved dearly and shared their homes, love and lives with, but I was a half-blood and this could never be! I wanted him so badly that I knew I if I had to stay here I would definitely grow as insane and messed up in the head like my Aunt Mayma.

I had to talk to my sister. I know she would sense my hesitation around Alisais the moment I tried to avoid him. I was never good at hiding anything from my sister in the past and surely as troubled as I was beginning to feel now with all my confused emotions, she would sense it immediately.

I lay there in the darkness and drifted off to sleep running the scenario of me explaining to my sister all the feelings I had, fearing how she may react in her fragile state. But she was my sister after all, and we always talked about everything and never kept secrets from one another.

Chapter 11

Morning came too soon. I knew what I must do no matter how much I dreaded it. Alisais had already headed out for the day with fresh frybread I had made in hand and my sister still lay silently slumbering all bundled in her bedding. Relieved that I could put it off a few moments longer, I headed out to gather the morning wood and milk the goat and bring my sister a fresh cup of milk to have with her morning meal. I figured I would talk to her while she ate, since lately her appetite had increased tremendously in the mornings and perhaps she would be more focused on her nourishment to comment much.

Fear and apprehension riddled my body that I shook near uncontrollably when I carried the milk and meal to my sister who had finally awakened and was sitting up awaiting me to join her. She scooted further up into a sitting position and thanked me, as I handed her the portions and headed back to the fire to retrieve hot water for my tea and return to her bedside to start the talk, I was not looking forward to having with her.

I hoped she was still to groggy to notice my trembling, but realized as I began to sit on the stool next to her, that I had trembled so violently when I handed her the milk moments before that half of it has spilled all over her. I felt terrible. My sister grabbed my trembling hand and placed it in hers and proceeded to ask me if I was okay.

I denied her suspicion of any issues and looked away to hide the tears welling up in my tired and swollen eyes from the long restless night before. When she inquired of me again as to my state of mind and trembling and reminded me of our constant openness growing up and that we never lied to each other in the past, I immediately drew back my hand and covered my face and sobbed.

How could I share with my sister all the mixed emotions I had?

How could I tell her, especially in her fragile state, just how much I was falling in love with her husband?

How could I tell her that I feel like I am betraying her and her kindness towards me with such feelings?

She began caressing my hair that had come loose from its braided bindings as she professed her accepting love for me no matter what the circumstances were that drove me to my current state of mind. I had been so disheveled that morning that I had forgotten to re-braid it when I woke up. I felt so distraught that I wished instead of her trying to comfort and tidy it, she would just rip it out of my head, so the pain on my scalp might outweigh the pain I was feeling in my heart that moment.

Laylah caressed my cheek, wiping away the tears and I could hold back the silence no more. Like a gust of wind it spewed out in a flurry. I told her everything. I also told her I was willing to take whatever punishment should befall me, and understood it was best that she banish me from her dwelling to quash my nonsense and feelings. It came out so fast and through the sobs that were so pronounced that I could barely catch my breath. In utter humiliation I threw my face down into her covers and continued to sob uncontrollably.

She then pulled me in close to her and placed her arms around my shoulder to comfort me. Wiping my tears and still hiding my face as I listened to her breathing and anticipating her response to be one of sisterly reprimand. That was not the case. I almost couldn't believe my ears when I began to hear her giggle softly as she grasped my chin to force me to look at her.

As my eyes met hers, I saw an unexpected smile on her face. She looked at me lovingly for a few seconds then said "welcome to womanly feelings and emotions". Then she explained that what I was experiencing was very normal once a young girl becomes a woman and starts noticing men and having feelings of longing. Even more surprising was her approval of my feelings and her expressing that it was acceptable and pleasing in her eyes that I would care for her husband as much as she did. She said "he was easy to love and it is natural to be attracted to a man so wonderful and loving".

I tried to choke back the tears as I reminded her that I am only a half-blood, and unworthy to be loved by anyone or love anyone. Still holding me close she wiped the tears from my eyes and uttered in soothing words, "my dear sister, times are changing among the people, and one day you will know the wonderful love I know".

Laylah did reprimand me for my stating that I was willing to be banished. She had a wrinkled and stern look on her face when she emphatically stated she would not hear me speak of such nonsense ever again! I was not to go anywhere and she would do no such thing. Under no uncertain terms would I be removed from her dwelling!

I loved her for loving me so much and understanding and I knew I would just have to focus on the tasks at hand and learn to control my wild desires and lusts somehow. Perhaps tossing my overheated hormones into a half frozen creek might help!

The next several days I did my best to focus on nothing more than the household chores of cooking, cleaning, mending, and collecting of firewood and water. I avoided Alisais as much as I could by waking as soon as I heard rustling about camp, so not to see him in the mornings. Then work as fast as I could during the daytime without stopping to take any breaks, so I could have supper done and retreat to my sleeping space alone before he came in the tipi for the night. No matter what I did, I still could not quench the burning desire deep within me.

No matter what attempt to avoid Alisais I chose, I could not seem to quit bumping into him at least a few times a day. It did become easier to cope with and he was around a lot less with the new treaties being presented to each tribe through the white men's negotiators visiting. Our whole camp seemed to be quite busy with the visiting natives from distant tribes choosing to have additional meetings to share their thoughts and suspicions of the white man's motives.

Some of them even spoke of uprooting their camps and families and traveling westward to avoid the tensions mounting along the Mississippi and Missouri rivers out east. Many nights Alisais and the other men could be heard in the distance sharing stories of the white men and their armies and the brutal ways towards our people and how they were promised peaceful resolutions, but all they had really noticed was the white men just wanted our furs and trade goods.

The savagery of their conversations as they talked of past years and the drunkenness that would follow these gatherings would scare me at times. It was a benefit though. By the time I started drifting off to sleep, I was too frightened to process any lustful thoughts for the images of bloodshed and death they spoke of had painted such revolting images in my mind.

I now understood why the women chose not to partake of these late night meetings and chats. Instead they chose to retreat to their tipis for the night and wait for their husbands to wander home in an intoxicated stupor sometime before sunrise. Which had become often since the white man introduced them to the vile poison that made men become bold idiots. It seemed the more they ranted, the more they drank, one fueled the other until they had little enough coordination or verbal skills to function and wandered home to sleep it off.

A few times when Alisais would return to the tipi, I would hear him stumbling around in his drunken state, knocking over pots, bowls and any other thing within the tipi that seemed, by his slurred accounts, to be "jumping out and intentionally attacking him", he would blurt out. I was happy for my sister that he usually did not drink as much as the other men and rarely came home without his wits intact. But on the occasions he did, it was quite entertaining.

I would giggle to myself and secretly watch him as he would clumsily wander about and sometimes carelessly remove his breech cloth, unaware anyone could see his foolish nakedness. How I had begun once again to be intrigued and attracted to him, despite the *devil in the jug* having taken hold of all his rational senses. I would silently flush, seeing what was secretively concealed beneath with a longing to explore its potential.

This thought I did not share with my sister, but knew she probably was aware, since she had caught me watching him with total adoration a few times. God how I hated she could almost read my mind at times. She would always just smile at me and nod when she caught me. How I longed so much now, to not only feel his touch again, but to be his.

~

I was no different than any of the other single women in our tribe, lusting after the pride of the pack so to speak!

Tall and well tanned, with long black locks of hair streaming past his shoulders, he had a body, that each time I saw him half unclothed, it nearly took my breath away. My heart ached to be his second wife, despite knowing it would never be.

It was uncommon that, any warriors at the age of twenty-seven, have only one wife, when many had at least four by the age of twenty-three. He had only one.

Every pure-blood female that had recently come to live in our camp in the last few weeks wanted to be his next pick and showed no shame in making it obvious. Their camp had come under attack several months back and there were almost no warriors left to protect them and with their Chief gone, they were left with no option but to merge with our camp for protection. There was always strength in numbers when attacks by unfriendly people came.

Alisais' appearance was not the first thing that drew me to him. It was his aura, his essence and his power within, that caught my attention. The way he loved my sister so tenderly is what hooked me. I felt as If I were pulled into a virtual vapor lock. like a moth to the flame in his presence. I was deeply drawn to him whenever I envisioned his likeness in the stillness of my thoughts.

Just his mere presence afflicted me with such commanding desire for submissiveness that it was hard to control my urge to do something, *anything* to draw his gaze towards me. It was if my body was wanting to scream, "here I am, take ME!" But I knew I could not ever reveal my feelings, it would expose my identity. Surely his mother would question my origins more deeply and have me exposed for the deceitful wretch I was to defile her son's home with half-blood filth she despised. No matter, I still could not quench my thirst for so much more with him.

With his every move he made I was longing for his intense brown eyes to penetrate my flesh as if to burn a hole into my soul leaving me breathless with such carnal desire and inconceivable lust. I longed for him to look upon me with the same caring and kindness he did my sister. I put the foolish thoughts aside and focused on my daily chores and continuing to make clothing and little trinkets for my soon to arrive niece or nephew to pass the time. I knew his parents would never approve of him having any relationship with the hired help, and he would never go against his parents wishes.

Every evening I longed more and more to be loved and have the emptiness in my life filled by someone special one day. This night was no different. We had heard talk all day of new soldiers possibly coming through with missionaries to convince those in poor health to travel with them to their camps and get some modern medicine by their doctors in hopes of a better life if they gave up our *savage* ways of life.

Knowing how much this enraged the Chief and other elders, we anticipated another long night of the men gathered in the Chiefs tipi drinking and cursing the very idea of leaving what was rightfully our land to bow to the ways of the very people who were stealing it from us.

I climbed into the bedding next to my sister to massage her aching and swollen legs so she could rest while Alisais was off attending to drinking and discussions in the tipi of his parents on the other side of the encampment. There was still a while before the baby was to come, but she seemed to be struggling and became weaker in the past few days. Her legs began to swell more often the last day or two and I knew it was hard for her to sleep with such discomfort.

She was also becoming more irritated with her husband's persistent affections during his drunkenness and as I started to rise and head to my own bed had asked me to lay there with her tonight. She said when Alisais returned, he would choose to sleep elsewhere because there would be no room for him. This had happened one other time when she was feeling bad and I had stayed close to her through the night and he had not objected. She hoped it would work again tonight, and I didn't mind. I would do anything to make her feel better and get well needed rest.

Laylah loved her husband dearly, but with the discomfort of the baby, and feeling still so nauseous all the time, she just didn't feel up to meeting the sexual appetite and desires of her husband. She even jokingly made reference to making me take her place one night if he became to intoxicated to notice, just so she could have a break. I laughed it off as her just being humorous and nothing more. I didn't know if ALL men were this way, but if they were, I now understood why they usually took a second wife. It was to give the first wife a break!

~

I must have drifted off into a deep restful sleep. So tired from working as hard as I could to keep up with my expected tasks and avoidance of Alisais efforts, that I had put myself in a state of total exhaustion. The it happened. I was abruptly awakened to the familiar sounds of a drunk trying to wander blindly through the tipi with no sense of balance or direction.

This time he truly must have had far more than ever before to drink, because he was singing old nursery rhymes to himself, slurring words and laughing as I could hear him fall over things, hit the floor, scurry back up and apologize to whatever he stumbled over for being so rude as if he were talking to other people. I dared not open my eyes for fear of giggling out loud and angering him while he was in such a state of confusion.

Several more moments of his drunken clumsiness,

singing and laughter filled the air in the tipi, and I had started to hold my breath so I wouldn't burst out in gut splitting laughter at the childish behavior he was displaying. I took a deep breath and squeezed my eyes tighter, trying to block the mental images of his appearance in that condition out of my head.

Fearing his noisiness might have awakened my sister, I gently slid my hand over to try and touch my sister laying next to me only to discover, she was not there. I panicked, only to open my eyes and notice Alisais hovering over me. In the darkness he stood there with a drunken smile on his face, slurring his words and protesting his undying love for me.

He moved in closer and stood right over me peering down with such fervor I felt I might self-combust right then and there. Truly the alcohol had gotten the best of all his wits, because he showed no sign of knowing that it was not his wife he was now drooling over, but her half-blood sister he was attempting to woo in the late hours of the night.

As I scrambled to get out of his way, and struggled to focus enough in the darkness to scan the room for my sister, He grabbed me up into his arms. "Where are you going my pretty little one", he belted out of his drunken mouth". I almost fell to the ground from the intoxicating smell of that white man's brew, that made the tribesmen get utterly stupid.

If I were a match, he would have gone up in flames for sure, but I didn't care! At the same time that my body was growing deep with desire for this I was also frantically looking about for my sister to see what had happened to her, and why she was not laying there with me. While trying to quell my growing desires I glanced over to my bedding along the far end of the tipi and saw her.

I glanced over to my sister, with a confused look, and knew she could understand what was going through my mind. When had she gotten up and moved to my bedding? My mind reeled back to her comment earlier, as I dangle in this drunken mans arms, and the fleeting thought that perhaps my sister had intended for this to happen all along, flooded my head. I tried to blink my eyes to see if this was a dream. It was not.

I looked back again at my sister and as our eyes locked. She gave me an approving nod and a look I had never seen before. She smiled, nodded again, blew me a kiss, laid back down and turned her head away from me as she pulled the covers further up over her. It was as if she were giving me her approval, and I was rapidly becoming locked in the moment.

Knowing the darkness of the night and his mental state, he would be oblivious to my identity, I could no longer hold back my desires.

I looked up again at Alisais, noticing the fire in his eyes, the lust in his soul, and knew I felt the same. As shameful as it was for me to not reject him, because he was most likely too intoxicated to be aware I was not worthy by tribe standards to be with him, I did not care.

I WANTED him.

I NEEDED him.

Tonight I would have him.

This moment, this night, I was going to experience what I had only dreamed of having. Someone to treat me like a woman, and make love to me. Even if he was totally drunk, I did not care. He was to have his way with me and my sister was well aware of and approved of it, and I was going to let it happen, no matter the consequences.

Chapter 12

With the gentleness of a dove he laid me back down and proceeded to caress my face and neck, kissing me ever so gently on the lips as he lowered himself to join me. I no longer cared about the smell of the intoxicating brew on his breath, because the intoxication of his tenderness had me spiraling with longing and desire. I felt as if I were a block of ice baking in the August sun as I melted beneath his caress, as he leaned closer into me.

With each tender kiss, I felt his gentle fingers inching downward along my night clothes, taking gentle caution to unfasten each tie gracefully as he planted kisses one after another. Even in his drunken state he was full of tenderness and affection. Fearing his eyes would eventually adjust to the poor lighting and he might come to his sense and punish me harshly for allowing him to be deceived, I started to make a feeble attempt to protest.

I could scarcely recognize the faint squeakiness in my voice as I tried to speak, when he suddenly pressed a finger to my lips and whispered softly, "I want you, let me have you tonight my love".

I must have lost all common sense, and thought of

consequence at that moment, because before I knew it, that strange, lustful person inhabiting my body took over. I gently wrapped my arms around him and I replied, gasping in sheer lust and willingness;

"YESS…TAKE ME".

His touch was as gentle as I envisioned it would be so many times in my dreams as I laid alone each night over the past few months. The desire and passion I felt to be in this moment with him, was as beautiful as I pictured it would be.

I gripped him even tighter with my arms and began to return tender kisses along his neck and chest as he began to slowly and methodically shed every stitch of clothing off of me in a quick swoop like a vulture snatching its prey. My excitement mounted as his kisses grew deeper, and I began to feel the hardness under his breech cloth grown immense against my hip.

"I have wanted to touch every inch of you for several days now but have resisted". "From your lovely long locks to the bottoms of your beautifully soft gifts of love.", he muttered softly. I panicked for a moment, what if he noticed my tummy was nowhere near the size he was accustomed to my sister having? Then he muttered again, "you are the angel sent from the Great Spirit to quell my loneliness and longing", then I knew he must have been so intoxicated he was living some imaginary dream he had concocted in him mind. I still did not care. If he was drunk enough to love me this night, and not remember me in the morning what harm would it cause to indulge myself and him as well, taking the burden of meeting his playful lusts away from my approving sister who lay nearby and fully aware of his intentions and my want.

He lay next to me, leaning over to continue caressing and kissing me as he babbled inaudible connotations of pleasure and desire. I reached over to feel beneath his breech cloth and seek to touch what I had only seen at a distance once before. This seemed to please him greatly as he shifted to remove the restraining materials to grant me momentary access. Then he gently maneuvered himself above me and was now resting on his knees straddling my waist.

The air began to feel intoxicating and my desires rose. Grasping my breasts, he began to gently lick and suckle them until I could no longer hold back the urge to buck my hips upward towards his erection in a spontaneous plea for him to take me.

"Take ALL of me NOW", I pleaded.

He continued to whisper soft words to me as I felt him gently part my thighs and slide his fingers upward to find my steaming wanton mound. My body was begging for him to breech the sacred spot only I have had the pleasure of exploring before.

Slowly and gently he inserted his fingers in and out of me as he kissed me, he whispered;

"You are truly a virgin sent to me from the Gods, this night."

"Tell me you want this as much as I want you".

"Tell me you want me here…."

he demanded as he thrust his fingers deep within me and gently wiggled them around until I let out a squeal and replied;

"YESSS, with a hiss.

With the quickness of a fox diving into his den, he thrust himself deep inside me and paused. His thickness hit me instantly, and I was lost in a haze of the terse pain and sensual pleasure at the same time. He held my cheek with one hand and whispered;

"I am sorry if I hurt you".

"We can go slowly",

he said as he proceeded to caress and kiss me again gently. Despite the painfulness of his invasion, I began to feel more and more aroused with his gentle, slow inward and outward movement. The caressing of my innermost sacred space had created a feeling so pleasurable, I couldn't think of a coherent word to describe the blessed feeling it gave me. I started to move in rhythm with him, savoring more of the wonderful excitement within me that was washing the initial shock of his penetrating pain from my mind.

With each thrust he inflicted I felt such an overwhelming urge to cry out loudly and beg for more as I felt my body start to fall into a sensation of ticklishness, pleasure and uncontrollable spasms all at once. I then began to feel him thrust harder, faster, over and over, as if he was able to read my mind. He let out a groan followed by a sigh, as he collapsed atop of me, out of breath and panting. Still trembling with such pleasure that the heaviness of him pressing down on my seemed weightless. Then he rolled off of me and took up a position on my side, looking up towards the top of the tipi, where smoke from the fire was billowing out out through the vented opening.

We lay there for a few moments in silence. Just when he had started to slow his breathing and I thought he had drifted off to sleep, he leaned into me again and began gently stroking my nipples and kissing my neck and shoulders.

Still out of breath and reeling from the earth shattering explosion that came from between my thighs just moments ago, I felt the warmth of his erection mounting against my thigh. I squealed playfully as he grabbed me firmly, flipped me over and drew me up onto all fours and thrust deep into me once again. This time he was not slow and merciful to my newness, and continued to thrust in and out much harder and faster than before.

The pain was quickly masked by the raw pleasure I was feeling built up inside with each new thrust. His groping hands flicked at one of my nipples when he reached his arm around to taunt its swelling tip. I was in ecstasy. I truly had died and gone to heaven. Someone was having as much pleasure with me as I was having with them! We soon both found our sensational release and collapsed into each other's arms exhausted. I lay there content as I watched him drift off to sleep.

~

The sun was peeking through the front bear skinned flap of the tipi when I awoke the next morning, rubbing my eyes, and realizing that last night was not a dream when I saw Alisais still sleeping next to me in the bed that belonged to him and his wife, not me. I looked at him then back at my sister across the room and quickly crept out from under the coverings and went over to join her. She was already awake and sitting on a stool preparing some tea, humming to herself and smiling. It was nice to see her feeling good that morning.

She and I talked little about the night before. The being loved and being made love to was wonderful, but the feeling of pain I had that morning was awful. I was not sure if it was normal, or just some Spirit punishing me once again for a deceitful act I had committed. I started to squirm from the discomfort and my sister suggested a remedy to ease the ache I felt and reassured me that was normal for the first time or two and that it would subside, and not be an issue in the future if I were to have the experience again of having an intimate relationship with a man.

She inquired if I was angry with her for putting me in such a situation without warning and I reassured her that I was more concerned that she might have regretted doing so. She confirmed her pleasure in sharing her husband with me. She said it was "like killing two birds with one stone". I was giving her husband what he needed, and she was allowing me to have an experience I craved as well. In a sense she was absolutely correct, I just was nervous that this trickery might be found out.

We talked a little more as she ate and once again thanked me for last night and allowing her to get some much needed sleep without disturbance. I felt it should be me groveling and being thankful! It was her who shared her husband with me, to fulfill my crazy lusts, putting her marriage and future at risk, should it ever be discovered what we had done.

We agreed that we both must remain silent and let her drunken husband awaken to assume that his night was all a dream. Even though we were sure he was too drunk to remember, we agreed we would pretend we knew nothing should he inquire. If he did question his night and wonder, we could claim that it must have been that awful *devil in a jug* giving him hallucinations.

We could not let him know he had been bedded with a half-blood. His father would surely take away his rightful place as the future leader of the people if word got out he slept with someone unworthy in his father's eyes. And what would be my sister's fate for having a hand in it? We vowed to keep the secret to ourselves. Deep inside my sister and I both knew that it was meant to happen and one day we would understand why the Great Spirit allowed that moment to be so.

Chapter 13

Three weeks passed since my late-night encounter with Alisais and not a single word had been mentioned about the liaison. I was relieved. I hadn't felt much like coping with any conflict that might arise, with my sister having more complications carrying her child. I was starting to feel a bit under the weather with some crazy prairie virus of late, and it seemed to sap all my energy out of me most mornings and leave behind a queasiness that surely would be comparable to a wild dog eating a tainted carcass.

The medicine man was coming almost daily to visit Laylah. He would dole out remedies and concoctions for her to consume. It seemed as if her weakness increased as each hour passed then she began to have fainting spells and more back pain. He demanded she stay in bed at all times, and called for some of the elder females to come and say prayers and chants to ward off the bad Spirit that may be causing the difficulties she was experiencing.

I sat dutifully by her side as often as I could to look after her, which became taxing with all the other tasks I had imposed on me by her mother in law, who still seemed to suck the air clean out of me any time she came around. I think my sister was annoyed by her overbearing and bossy ways as well, because she would fain sleep whenever her voice came within earshot of the tipi.

Day in and day out I started my morning, by dousing my face in the cool creek before collecting water to take back to the tipi. It seemed to momentarily stop the awful feeling of nausea that I would succumb to so early each day. I had to put how ill I felt out of my mind as Laylah was growing weaker each day. There were times when she would awaken only to take a sip of water and a small morsel of food before drifting back off to sleep.

My ill condition was surely just the Great Spirit was punishing me for the deceitful rendezvous I had with my sister's husband that one night. I could think of no rational cause for such a lengthy illness other than that. I suppose it was less of a punishment that I be reminded each morning of the *bed of betrayal* I laid in, than him remembering it and reprimanding me harshly and who knows what!

I had just finished filling several gourds and put them on the yoke heading up the embankment, when I was stopped suddenly in my tracks by the loud yells from Alisais who had just emerged from the tipi. "Someone fetch the medicine man and hurry, the baby, the baby, something is wrong, the Spirit has come for him", he yelled frantically, before darting back into the tipi.

I dropped the yoke and the gourds tumbled back down the banks behind me, spilling out all their contents as they careened back to the banks where I had just filled them.. I hurriedly made my way inside the tipi to kneel beside my sister. My own head swimming from my nausea, I almost toppled onto her as I grasped her hand and felt the cold clamminess of her waning grip.

I sat there wiping her forehead with a cool cloth as she cried and choked for air wrenching in pain as blood pooled around her in the bed. The nurse maid who always tended to the mothers giving birth had arrived moments before me and was pacing frantically saying "the baby was not coming proper". "Surely she would die of blood loss if they did not get the baby out of her", she said emphatically. Alisais was coaxed out of the tipi by his mother, because if the baby was to come today, the father's were not to be around for that part. A man could sure help a woman get into such a predicament, but they were never around for the taxing experience of birthing their offspring, another oddity in tradition that could breed bad results.

~

Tradition dictated, they can spread their seed and

make the babies, but they don't stick around to bring them into the world. Any part of the deliveries, and post care a woman needs, a husband would have no part of dealing with for fear of bringing the new infant bad luck in development.

As if a voodoo curse were to strike them dead if they were to hang around, the men always vanished when a baby was about to be born. Once the babies were birthed and the mother and infant relocated to the home of her mother for aftercare for several weeks, only then would they reunite with one another to acknowledge their offspring and formally name them.

This was tradition, and Dare-be-it for Alisais to defy his mothers coaxing away and word get back to his father! Then there was his mother and the repercussions of defying superstition, since she could be as vengeful as a rattlesnake cornered between rocks in a searing desert sun. I could see it in his eyes, he was pained and he wanted to stay by Laylah, he loved her so much.

~

The medicine man arrived with his trusty bag of trinkets and toxins as I called them. Some of them tasted awful and the collection of things he used in his chants and rituals were just plain eerie, or smelled of death themselves.

He said the baby was coming early and struggling, I then knew it was time to run down to the east camp where my mother still lived among the workers, and fetch the many cleaned rags she had started to gather months before in preparation as all mothers do for when their daughters bear children. Momma gathered them up and came with me. This would be her first time coming to the tipi of my sister and her husband.

Another odd custom I didn't understand much. A mother-in-law was not to be in the presence of her daughter's husband. After marriage, she was his relation now, and outside of this wife occasionally visiting her sisters and parents, there was a severance of most ties. She was however, expected to be the one to provide the nurturing care needed by a new mother and her infant the first month of their bonding and healing.

Momma and I arrived back and joined the others gathered around my sister, as the medicine man chanted, burned incense and administered some tea to my sister in a cup. This was to help ease the pain as her child struggled between birth and the netherworld he proclaimed the Spirit was trying to take him into. As my sister tried to swallow the first few sips, she began to choke and then vomited all over the side of the bedding and swore that she would rather die than drink something that tasted a vile as horse excrement.. The medicine man added a few sweet root and berries to it and she was able to get a few sips in without it spewing back out like someone expelling bad Spirit out after a cleansing ritual.

The night fell fast, then morning came, still no child had been born. Laylah laid there motionless and as pale as a white cloud against a stormy black sky. There were sounds of wailing off in the distance as some of the other elders wives were chanting a few tipi's over and I knew this couldn't be good. The medicine man said the evil Spirit brought by the white man had stolen the child from among the people as punishment for our doing trade with them in the past. He made preparations to remove the lifeless infant from my sister's womb.

I held my sisters' hand in mine as I felt her draw air deep into her lungs and succumb to the world beyond as she let out her very last breath. Her soul was now ascending upon the great white buffalo and into the heavens to join her son.

I did my best to hide the tears that began to stream down my face. I did not want to let go of her hand. My only sister, the one who understood me better than anyone, my best friend, was now gone. I could not openly grieve the loss, or our secret would be discovered. It was hard enough that my mother just lost her eldest daughter, she did not need the fallout of our deceit to destroy her completely.

Chapter 14

My mother and I were tasked with the preparing of my sisters body for ritual burning to release her soul to the heavens. It was decided by the tribal council that the whole dwelling would be burned as well to remove any lingering bad Spirit that might be present. Alisais would move back to the tipi of his parents to grieve, since he had no other wives and I would return to my mother's place on the far side of the creek with the rest of the workers and half-bloods.

Holding in my overwhelming grief, so not to expose the secrets that would go to the heavens with my sister's soul and fighting the urge to not spew the contents of my stomach as a result of whatever ailed me became a task I was rapidly failing at. After my mother and I completed our task, we headed back to the lower camp and spent our evening grieving alone with my aunt.

My sisters body laid with her sons in the tipi with the medicine man and an elder who would spend the night saying prayers for the evil that overcame them would ascend into the depth of the nether-world when their Spirit passed to the heavens with ancestors. I didn't care too much for the thoughts that an evil spirit is what was claimed to take the life of my sister or her son, and became even more ill and worried about what kind of spirit was taking hold of me to make me succumb to such odd sickness I had been feeling lately as well. I lay there trying to smother myself in blankets and fur to try and bury the feeling that perhaps part of my deceit was the cause of my sisters demise. How could I live with myself if this was all my fault?

~

We stood outside our tipi that mourning, bidding our farewell to my sister from a distance, as several tribesmen set a blaze the tipi Laylah and Alisais once called home and bid my sister and her baby's soul a last good-bye. Like a torch to my soul, my heart burned with grief. It took every inch of strength I could muster to stand there without fainting. I could barely hold in the meager contents of my stomach as I watched. I wanted to be able to be closer, but we knew we couldn't risk someone drawing conclusions, since I was no more than the hired help in their eyes, and my mother just a camp worker, despite it being her child she lost, it was of little significance to the Chief and his family. Tears began streaming down my face, as I tried to let go of my sister, my best friend. Everything went a blur.

I came to, lying on my mother's bed, with her

fanning me and asking me how long I had been ill. I protested having any true illness so she wouldn't worry. I suggested that perhaps I felt so weak and frail because of the heavy work load that was placed on me while caring for my sister during the last month and that I had not eaten for nearly a day and a half. My aunt Mayma started rambling over in the corner where she was sitting and rolling dough for making frybread. She said "one bobbly gone and another bobbly to replace it" over and over again.

I tried hard to ignore her rambling and protested her repeated insistence as her being crazy while noticing my mother's face becoming quite ashen. Quickly moving over to the furthest part of my mother's tipi I busied myself straightening up bedding and trying to ignore them both and pretend this awkward moment would fade. I closed my eyes as tears welled up. It had just sunk in and I understood the reasoning behind her concerns.

How could I have not seen this possibility?

It couldn't be possible!

I wanted to die!

She gave me a stern look then turned her head away. Suddenly she rose up turning around then looking back at me. With panic in her eyes, she said,

"So it is true?"

I knew exactly what she was asking but thought, with the angry look in her eyes, playing dumb would be the best option about now.

I stood up to move towards her with an inquisitive expression on my face, when she slapped me, then blurted out,

"You lay with Alisais and are with child, are you not?"

Shock must have overcome me, because the only thing I remember before feeling my head hit the dirt with such force, was the spinning in the room that crept up on me as soon as those words passed her lips. I had fainted again.

Tears once more began to flow from my already swollen eyes, as I questioned how that could be? I had only bedded with him one night. Mother then proceeded to give me a full crash course in the *'what's and how's'* of procreation. Was this to be my demise for all the deceitful action I had partaken of in the past year?

Mother told me she had a dream last night, and the Spirit visited her in those dreams, giving her visions of me bearing the child of a great warrior that would one day lead our people, but this was far from what she had in mind. She looked now as pale as a November sky and sank to the ground herself in disbelief and tears. She was worried for my life and for my future. As mean as the Chief was at times when it came to honoring tribal traditions and his disdain for half-bloods, this could really get ugly.

She was also afraid because she was getting older in years, that if her participation were to be revealed, or that if anyone knew I was pregnant with the future Chiefs son, by behaving deceitfully, I could possibly be stoned to death, and left for the crows to pick my bones on some hill far in the distance. There would not be any relations left to care for my momma when she could no longer care for herself either. We both felt the doom that possibly loomed in our futures.

I moved closer to my mother and we embraced. Occasionally we peered out the front of the tipi to still see the smoldering of the burning that was my sister and her son retreating to the heavens and the scurrying of other workers completing daily tasks and preparing a few food items to take to the main camp to feed those in mourning the tribes loss. I ached inside because part of me still felt so much love and compassion for Alisais and knowing now I would never get to be in his presence again being my sister had passed and I was no longer needed.

We spent the rest of the day inside nestled together as I explained the circumstances around Alisais and my encounter and trying to decide how we would get through this alive. I told my mother how I felt and that I loved him very deeply and could not deny that feeling and that there was absolutely nothing I would do to cause any harm to the child I was carrying even if I had to flee our camp to keep the secret. The reality of the situation became a concern when we realized I only had a certain amount of time before people would question my condition that would be visibly evident. I knew my mother and aunt had told everyone in the reclaimed camp that I had been snatched by white men and hauled off, but what would we say about my return?

We could tell them I was abandoned in the woods after being violated and they might accept that, but the moment I gave birth, and the child began to show his features, would it be obvious he resembled some of the trademark features that Alisais' family all carried? Reassuring my mother the whole time that he had no recollection of that night, or at least I thought so, since it was never mentioned. We assumed perhaps we could pull it off.

~

A few weeks had come and gone and I was finally getting back to my old routine of collecting wood, fetching water and catering to the needs of the main tribal camp, who I had all but forgotten could be ten times needier than my sister and her husband were for no reason at all except they felt *entitled*.

How smug and demanding they were to our kind

and I sure did not miss that one bit. By the end of each day I felt as if my back had been carrying the load of a work horse. My legs ached as if I had walked up and down a few rugged mountains like a pack mule carrying furs to trade in one of them white man's camps they called a village or town.

Each evening it took great effort to remove the moccasins from my aching and swollen feet. The nausea seemed to fade as each day passed, but was now replaced by the weight I was gaining and the lack of energy I had. I was even more content that no one seemed to be the wiser to my condition or to the small increase in my belly size under my loosely fit deerskin dress. Everyone was busy working Mother Earth and turning her outer core in preparation for seeding a new season of crops to harvest in a few months.

My mother and I kept to ourselves more than we had in the past. I truly believe she was more afraid of losing me as she did my sister, than her rapidly failing heath that seemed to keep her bedridden most days. Aunt Mayma had quit her ramblings about me being with child and kept busy picking up the slack for my mother.

Some of the other women in our *reclaimed* encampment frequently visited in on her and shared stories while I was off working and she would have such hope and excitement in her voice as she would retell them to me in the evenings. I still missed my sister, but enjoyed so much the company of my mother which I had lost out on while up in the main camp.

I enjoyed hearing her talk of the affairs of the camp, the talk of changes one day as trade seemed to increase and bring new things to our people. I also enjoyed her telling me stories of her childhood and how she had met her husband so long ago. She spoke of the day he gave her the beautifully beaded moccasins I was privilege to wear while working for my sister that his mother made. I no longer wore them, since my feet had swollen so much they no longer fit. It seemed that almost nothing was fitting lately.

I labored as fast as I could each day just so I could end my day sitting by her side. Listening to the gossip overheard in conversations taking place within the walls of the Chief's tipi were our only way to really know what was going on outside of the rare tribal meetings. I wondered how accurate the news was. By the time I heard it, many a person had added their own interpretation and annotations.

The rumor mill was usually the only way we were kept informed of what was happening or what was to come of the future of our people and the many tribes out on the Plaines. The only time we were called to gather at any of the tribal meetings would be to clarify possible hardships ahead and what was expected of us. We were usually dismissed before any deeper discussions or decisions were made and not privy to the real truth and plans for our camps. Nor were we allowed to attend the other functions, dances and celebrations that sometimes followed.

I recalled many the conversations my sister and I would have during the day and in the evenings when Alisais was away. She talked of all the changes he wanted to make among the camp after his dad passed and he would be the one making decisions for the best of our people. I wondered if he would ever follow through with what he had told her and she shared with me, or would his grief continue to drive him to give in to continuing the older ways of his father.

The ladies would talk down by the banks of the creek often and I had heard them referred to Alisais as *Crazy Feathers* since he had become so withdrawn and acted strangely. I tried not to listen to what they rambled about, but knew I had better never linger close in their presence as my belly had begun to grow more rapidly and I grew angry over some of their mocking a man my sister loved and I still loved deeply as well. Secrets, all these secrets, would I ever escape my inner turmoil?

Most of the women just scoffed when they saw me and turned their backs away in my presence anyway. Not only was I a half-blood, but I was a half-blood who was defiled by a white man and was cursed as much as my mother was, times two! I just decided to avoid any confrontation and rude remarks, I would just wait until they were having their afternoon meal to collect water, do washing and then bathe in the darkness of the night to keep my sanity.

Chapter 15

Six and a half more grueling months had passed. My belly was protruding and the wee one kicking at my innards every moment it could, as I continued to work and care for my mother in the evenings as she was now all but confined to staying inside due to her bones aching her so.

No one questioned my condition. I had learned that my aunt had told everyone that I was returning from the main encampment when I was attacked by some wandering drunken Native savage from another tribe and he had his way with me. That was more a relief than them thinking I was carrying the child of a white man.

I sometimes chuckled to myself, as I thought of her explanation for me being with child. Yes, Alisais, was a savage alright! A savage romantic at that! And he did have his way with me, but I welcomed it with every fiber of my existence because deep inside my heart, I still loved him. With that thought in my mind, I found my happiness and peace.

I was happy and no one would take that happiness from me, even if I had to hide my secret truth. The more my child moved around inside my belly, the happier I felt. I knew he would be a blessed child because my sister was in the heavens, watching over us. I would see her sometimes in my dreams telling me that one day everything would be well and that the child I carried would one day be a great leader, and I would find peace among the people. I wished for those words I heard her speak in my dreams, but still kept guarded, because I knew no matter what I thought, it usually never matched the end results of my reality. Bad luck seemed to follow me like a bobcat chasing a rabbit for a noontime snack.

~

Harvest time was near its end. The time for my wee one to arrive had come. It wasn't long after I felt that first twinge of pain that my child breathed the first breath of air letting out a holler that would have knocked an owl out of a tree. A boy, just as I saw in my dreams.

He was breathtakingly beautiful. He was a healthy boy with jet black hair and deep brown eyes just like his father. As I glanced at him and all his perfection, I noticed he even bore the small eagle shaped discolored birthmark on his right upper thigh, just like his father and his father's brother. This would have to remain hidden if I were to keep my secret as to his lineage. I snuggled up in my bedding after my aunt and momma had finished fussing over me, and drifted off to sleep with my most precious treasure sleeping while cradled in the crook of my arm, happy.

I spent a few weeks recovering and knew it was time to head back out to help with the last of the harvest. If I didn't pull my weight in the toils and labors of the harvest the shunning and animosity it might create could cause complications and result in me being put out of the camp. Toting my son strapped into a cradleboard fashioned by my aunt and tethered on my back, I headed out to start my work.

I couldn't be happier looking into my sons eyes every time I glanced up to see him peering back at me as he was propped up where I could see him as I worked. I sang to him often to pass the time, and work didn't bother me as long as I had my beautiful son with me. Each time I looked into his eyes I was also saddened that he would never know his true father and the family that was his, and his birthright. But knowing he was half the blood of a man I had grown to admire and love from afar was special.

I would close my day by cuddling him, happy that I was blessed with such a special gift to love, that was all my own. I enjoyed the interaction my mother had with him as well. It was nice to listen to my mother sing him to sleep as I prepared her evening meals and helped her ready herself for sleep. She may have been bed ridden, but she seemed so overjoyed with his presence, that every evening she insisted she get to have those personal and heartwarming moments with him. She felt that the dangers of keeping our secret and fear of reprimand dissipated whenever those beautiful brown eyes of his sparkled up at her as he cooed.

~

Alisais had spent the better part of the summer learning from his father more of the tribal responsibilities he would soon undertake. The negotiating of new agreements and making treaties with some of the white men for food in exchange for furs and trinkets that the tribe had plenty of and so on. He had also seemed quite troubled and distant at times. Some felt it was because the overwhelming changes brought about by the treaties Taft had tried to impose, but I knew it was much more than that.

I could sense it. I was not sure if it was my diluted illusion that maybe one day he and I could be together with our son, or perhaps he was still grieving the loss of my sister. Either way, when I lay to rest each night, I felt his discomfort, his pain, his longing. For what I was not sure. Nor could I understand why I was feeling it so. Sometimes it left me restless and unable to sleep. Each night I prayed to my ancestors that I would find answers, yet none came.

He had moved back out from his parent's tipi into a new one he had erected at the edge of the encampment right before the harvest season. I had heard it was because he wanted it placed as far away from where the one he shared with my sister had been set to ashes because it brought him horrible nightmares. People had begun whispering that perhaps one of the evil Spirit that had stolen his wife and son from him had started to take his mind from him as well. He was often seen wandering the camp, ranting to himself late at night, muttering something about the maiden that came to his dreams and stole his heart and soul before his wife died. He felt that it was his destiny to be with that maiden that came to him and lead the people of the tribe one day and that is why Laylah was taken from him.

~

There she would be standing next to him in his thoughts when he hunted, and again laying next to him in bed as he dreamed. He could not get her image out of his mind.

Who was this maiden that invaded the deepest recesses of this thoughts?

He felt there was something familiar about her, yet the only clear vision he could see, was those moccasins. Those beautiful hand beaded moccasins. He had no idea where he had seen them before, but they were familiar. He knew in his heart they belonged to the woman he wanted to spend the rest of his life with, and would go to his death alone if he could not have just her. So much of her resembled his wife past. What was it that made her seem so familiar?

Why could he not get her image out of his head?

Despite rumors of his possible insanity, his father, Chief Stumbling Bear believed in him. He had similar visions of his son with a woman and child late at night as well and began to inquire of his son about it.

Alisais shared with his father the dreams and visions. He said that he saw this woman in a dream, and she was to be the mother of his son, his wife. But he was troubled as to how he would find her, and how this would be. Little did he realize that she truly did exist and not only had she already been in his bed, but she had also bore him a son that he only dreamed existed. She was just across the creek from him all the many months, but if she had her way, he would never know!

The Chief was nearing the time he was to find his way into the next world and walk among the ancestors gone before. He no longer spent the majority of his time sitting outside by the main fire circle and in the presence of other elders. Instead they met more secretly behind the skins of his tipi in private pow-wows. Knowing his time was drawing close troubled the elders. They did not feel Alisais was up to the task of being Chief and the responsibilities that would encompass his role if his mental stability remained in question. They also felt it in order for Alisais to take the rightful place as the new tribal Chief, he must have a wife and child to carry on their legacy, their ways, and it must be soon. Silently I wished it would be me, but knew that would never happen. Expectations and customs trumped love, and I could never compete with his stuck-on-tradition family.

Late that afternoon Chief Stumbling bear called for all the elders to gather together and meet him in his tipi for an urgent matter that needed attending to. It was then he announced to them that his son was not possessed with a bad spirit that passed from his wife, but had been having visions from the great Spirit. He also proclaimed that the Spirit had been coming to him in visions as well, relaying the same predictions. Soon he and his bride would be found, and they were tasked with locating her.

Chief Stumblingbear said that every warrior in the camp must help in the hunt for this woman. Alisais explained what he had seen in his dreams and as he explained how she appeared and the moccasins, some of the warriors began to look at each other and back at him. When he inquired as to their expressions of confusion and curiosity, they relayed to him that the description was familiar to them as well, but they were not sure why. Could it be that it was someone they had seen visiting their camp from a nearby tribe?

Either way, they were to set out at first light and search for her from sunrise to sunset until she is found. Once again reminded of her appearance and the moccasins they all made mental notes and agreed after glancing at the Chiefs pleas for help in his weakened state, that the matter was very urgent.

He demanded all the men must search every tipi, hut and lean-to in the camp and surrounding camps at once. They were to also search everyone's belongings and tipis for the moccasins. The chief feared someone could be hiding them to disguise the maidens existence as an attempt to overthrow his camp for being defiant of some of the newer happenings in other camps and adhering to the deep hatred he had for the white man and changes. Little did he know his son was all for some of those changes.

No place could be overlooked and no camp exempt. They must find her, the owner of those moccasins at once if his son was to take his rightful place as Chief before he died. At sunrise the next morning, the men would start their search for this woman.

It did not take long for word of the hunt for this beaded moccasin maiden hit the camp of the *reclaimed* as well. Right on to my ears it fell like an axe to a parcel of wood to be splintered for kindling, with such force and violence I shook in utter fear. Perhaps he had remembered their night together much more than he let on. Perhaps he knew it was the girl who helped his wife and that he bed with in a drunken moment of lust one night, and just revealed it as a dream, so not to shame his family for consorting with the help or not choosing to marry a second wife. Whether he truly remembered or not, the fear of being found out as a half-blood and my true identity being exposed frightened me more than anything in the world.

I rushed immediately back to our tipi and explained to my mother what I had come to know by eavesdropping and that we had to hide the moccasins immediately! They would discover my deceit and I would be punished harshly.

What would happen to my son?

Would he be taken from me then what about me?

Would I Possibly be put to my death?

I could not risk having my son taken away from me. He was the most precious thing I had come to have since losing my sister. He was my "Little Bird" I named him that because of the song he put in my heart when he smiled. He made me happier than I had ever been.

I would die before she let anyone take him from me!

Not only would we have to hide the moccasins, but my mother and I also feared he may recognize me and the slight resemblance to my sister that I bore, might draw some of the main camps warriors attention. For the safety of my mother, myself and my son, I must flee the camp as well.

Chapter 16

I trembled and cried as I hugged my mother around the neck, then kissed her and told her goodbye. We knew I had to flee the camp if I was to spare us any harm. I had to take my chances upon the prairie and try to get to one of the missionary camps further east that the white men had opened in old Shawnee that we had heard about.

The missionaries we had heard of took in many native women and their children who had nowhere to go. They did this in hopes to spread their ways and beliefs and attempt to reform our *savage ways of the devil.* I could play their game and pretend to be reformed. I had after all spent the last year getting good at being deceitful. I was sure at least that I would live and be with my son. Nothing else mattered as long as I had him.

I hated seeing the pain in my mother's eyes as I glanced at her. But we both knew, I was a half-blood that had deceived the tribe; if I stayed I would surely die. It was growing dark and the men had not made it to our camp yet and were up resting by the fire with intent to continue their search in the morning of one more local camp and then search our camp. I would leave in the middle of the night so the cover of darkness would hide me from view in case they were keeping a watchful eye for anyone sneaking about.

I went and packed a few things in a small bag fashioned from skins I had made to carry berries I planned to pick this fall. It was just big enough to hold a few pieces of clothing for my son, some dried jerky and an old knife mom gave me. Looking back at my mother as she had drifted off to sleep from worry and exhaustion, I saw her raise her hand up into the air and call out her parents names, begging of them to watch out for me, and to welcome her into the heavens with them should her pain be too unbearable with me gone.

I knew this would be hard for her after losing my sister, and was at least slightly comforted my aunt was here with her. She may be crazy, but she was kind and caring and would look after my momma for me. It was late, I had to finish readying and head out. Sunrise would come in a few hours, and I had to slip away unnoticed. I put my son in his cradleboard and headed out into the darkness. The minimal lighting from the moon in the cloudy fall sky was a welcome relief in keeping me from being seen, but offered no hope of me not hurting myself as I sped across the fields to get to the wooded tree lines before morning light took to the sky. It was unusually warm and humid. If this was any inclination on what the day would be like when the sun came up I knew I could not travel far before exhaustion would set in.

I wanted to put as much distance between me and our camp as I could. As I started running closer to the trees along the hills, I could feel the warmth in the air picking up. I had been walking fast for a few hours, tripping over bushes and rocks on the uneven ground in the darkness and felt I needed to seek some kind of shelter to wash the scratches and cuts I had acquired in my frightful fleeing. Little Bird had become restless and I knew that to keep from falling victim to the heat about to take hold, and both of us needing nourishment soon, we must to take shelter swiftly and rest. I could travel again at night when it was cooler.

~

It was sunrise and once again the Chief, Alisais and many elders were talking over their continued plans to leave no stone unturned, no tipi un-tossed until they laid eyes on either the moccasins or the maiden who bore the description of whom Alisais was determined to have by his side, as his bride, and soon.

As soon as they finished a quick meeting, the warriors headed down to the camp of the reclaimed, searching and questioning everyone they could. Momma and Maya were glad when they were done having every bit of their personal belongings pilfered through and the men left their tipi. That relief was short lived when one of the other women who tended to dislike my mother started to run towards the warriors and declare she knew who they were hunting for. This woman had harbored ill feelings towards my mom since she had extra work to do as a result of my mother's poor health lessening her work abilities.

"She has a daughter with fancy moccasins", she blurted out. "I saw her wearing them just a few days past, she is a half-blood with a new child and the half-sister of Alisais wife who passed", she said as she continued motioning towards mommas tipi with a vengeful look in her eyes.

Immediately Alisais was summoned and the warriors headed towards momma's tipi in search of an explanation for the woman's ranting and to inquire about the allegations made.

~

Standing on the edge of the hillside working hard to catch my breath and find a good place to take shelter from the heat setting in, I looked back and noticed there was a commotion and loud noises being carried in the warm winds.

Having a sense of uneasiness, I started searching around in haste, for a quick place to hide. I found a resting place for us under a rocky overhang, well hidden by trees and brush where we could stay out of view should anyone look out in our direction and see me moving about. I needed rest, Little Bird was hungry and needed to be freed from the cradleboard and exercise his little restless and wiggly legs. This spot would have to do for now and I would wait here and rest until nightfall and it was safe to move on.

Pulling Little Bird from his bindings and nestling him in my arms as he nursed from my bosom, I ate some jerky and berries and gently stroked his silky black wisps' of hair between my fingers. Watching him and feeling the bond of love we shared, I knew no matter how uncertain our future together was, no matter the difficulties that may come, as long as his warm eyes and adorable smile were looking up at me, we would be okay. Nothing else mattered to me.

Soon his little tummy was full and he fell fast asleep. I made a soft pallet of what leaves and moss I could find taking care to move as little as possible. I laid him down and curled up around him to rest. Unaware of the impending doom that would abruptly awaken me shortly; I closed my eyes and fell victim to the lack of sleep that weighed on my weary body.

~

Momma and Aunt Mayma sat in their tipi with the warriors that had searched their place earlier and now standing perched outside, guarding them. The Chief arrived shortly with Alisais by his side as well as several other head elders from the main camp. They entered the tipi and the questioning began.

After long moments of yelling, followed by silence and the cycle of banter replaying over and over, They emerged from the tipi. Alisais and the Chief headed for the main camp and the warriors mounted their horses and headed off in the direction of the woods up near the hills an hour's ride off in the distance.

~

Startled awake by gruff voices, I opened my eyes to see two warriors from the main camp staring down at me in disgust. I was frightened almost motionless as I leaned over my son to shield him from them. Two of them were talking among themselves as the third one snatched my sons cradleboard up and motioned for me to hurry and strap him in it. I leaned over and softly placed a kiss on his forehead and tried to gently bundle him into it without waking him. I remember this man was one of the warriors who treated me harshly and spat on me when I was caught trying to sneak and see my sister on her wedding night and cringed.

The moment the last strap was fastened, he yanked the cradleboard up and slung the strap over his shoulder like my son was a dead carcass to be tossed and taken back to camp to be skinned. Little Bird began to wail as he was bounced around. I started to get angry and protest when the other man grabbed me like a sack of potatoes and threw me over his shoulder, dragging me from our hiding place kicking and screaming.

In an effort of resistance knowing it would be in vain I continued kicking and screaming to be let down..

This was not right, how could they do this?

How could they be so mean to my son?

How could they ignore him screaming to be comforted?

Were his cries falling on deaf ears?

I was angry as he mounted the horse and yanked me up with him, planting a harsh smack across the side of my tear stained cheek.. He verbally admonished me, telling me;

"Be silent and that I had disgraced my relations, I had nothing to say that he wanted to hear."

"The council would deal with you as they saw fit", he said gruffly.

Disgraced my relations? What was he talking about? Since when did anyone in the tribe really care about any *reclaimed*? We were after all the lower sector of the tribe, forced to live on the opposing side of the creek with the rest of the half-bloods and misfit crazies. How would disgracing my family affect them anyway? They didn't consider us their family, so what was their anger about? The look in his eye seared a hole clean through me and I fell silent, knowing that if I didn't, he might end my life right then. He had a look of pure hate and evil in his eyes.

This man was crazier than my Aunt ever was!

As My body lay draped over the ass end of the horse being bounced around until my gut ached, I felt it would be a relief to just fall off and be trampled by the horses than to spend another moment helplessly dangling and unable to comfort my sons wailing that continued to echo as we rode along.

Upon arrival at the main camp I was abruptly pushed off the horse and forced into one of the tipis next to the Chiefs. I tried to look back towards where my son was, and was immediately reprimanded for that action by a swift blow to the other side of my face. Reeling in pain, exhausted and resigned, I collapsed on the ground just inside the flap.

Everything swirled around me and I began to think it was my time, perhaps I was dying and a evil Spirit was coming to take me away to join my sister. My body began to shudder in pain and I proceeded to vomit what few contents were in my stomach and felt so parched from lack of water that my skin felt it had been set ablaze. I tried to sit up and focus, but did not have enough energy to even open my eyes. The pain was intense, all I could do was lay there on my side, in my own filth and wish that the Spirit would be merciful when they carried me away to whatever hell awaited me on the other side.

A few moments passed and the room around me came more into focus and I could once again make some sense of the conversation taking place between the two women who sat in front of me. They were chattering about how bad I appeared and smelled and proceeded to discuss what lay ahead once I came to.

Realizing I was not dying, and just suffering from lack of nourishment, exhaustion and pain, I closed my eyes and opted to lay there motionless a bit longer. I was hoping that I could catch a bit more of their conversation and have an insight to the repercussions of my deceitful actions and perhaps discover just how much they really knew and how they knew. I wanted an explanation for the accusations of betraying my family. What family besides my mother and aunt did I have? I had not shamed them. They understood and helped me leave for my own safety, that couldn't be considered betrayal with her blessing.

One of the two older women got up and kneeled beside me and began to shake me vigorously and curse as she forced me to a sitting position. The other woman joined her next to me as they proceeded to state that they must get me cleaned up and ready to face the council of elders.

They grabbed me by my hair and proceeded to hastily and with great reprimand, strip down my garments, wash and lather me with ointment that smelled revolting and put a new lamb-skin frock on me. Then demanded I eat and drink before I collapsed again. I needed to be in a good mental state before learning my fate, the shorter woman said, as she continued to poke my arm frequently telling me to hurry and eat.

I tried to speak only to be ignored as if they could not hear me. Cursing and mumbling to themselves right in front of me as if I were not even there they concurred as to what a disgrace I was to flee, and how the elders were outraged at my behavior.

Never once did they come right out and say what it was I allegedly did. I was so frightened, that I didn't know what to expect next. The one older woman turned to leave and instructed the other to restrain me if I attempted to leave. I sat there and glanced around. I had been so frightened, that I did not even notice my son was fast asleep in a small hammock just a few feet away. I felt relieved, but saddened, not knowing what was to come of us and our future together.

Chapter 17

My son now starting to waken and move about, I started to rise to tend to him and was yanked back down quickly. I begged her to let me remove him from the hammock to nurse and comfort him. She protested and said that she would bring him to me and that I was not to move from where I was sitting. "I don't trust you to not grab him and bolt for the woods", she stated as she picked him up and placed him in my arms. I felt like a trapped and caged animal like I once saw in one of the white man's books. The image of a tiger and her cub in a cage with the words "circus" written in fancy lettering below it came to mind.

I held my son close to me, sang to him, keeping my eyes closed the whole time, telling myself that if I just keep them closed, all of this would go away and I would wake up from this horrid nightmare soon. I sat there for what seemed like hours, and Little Bird had finally drifted off to sleep. My legs began to feel numb from not being able to walk around.

The woman took him from me and laid him back in the buckskin hammock then ordered me to eat more so I could regain strength and then rest. The council would be coming for me soon, but not until I had rested enough to be presentable to stand before them and accept my punishment. I was relieved that I had a little more time, but found resting a task almost impossible to achieve.

I felt like a rabbit captive in a trap as she sat between me and the entry way, while the other woman sat perched between my son and I. I wanted to desperately snatch him and flee, but knew in my heart, I must stay strong, and stay put, because I would go nowhere without my son. I must face whatever was to happen and hope they spare my life and the life of Little Bear.

Another full day had come and gone. The older woman had been gone for quite some time and the shorter, and a bit younger woman, who was much kinder offered me some tea as she sat next to me and gently brushed and re-braided my hair. She softly whispered that I was strong and brave and that I must put my trust in the Great Spirit that one day all would be well.

I pleaded with her to tell me what was going on and why I was being treated so awful. Just as I had finished my question, the other woman returned and she stopped fixing my hair and quickly retreated from the tipi. The older, harsher woman replied, "you have shamed your relations, shamed the tribe, and must be punished accordingly".

"How?" I protested.

In frustration over my persistence she explained that when the men went into the camps looking for Moccasins belonging to the maiden that Alisais had seen in his dreams, a woman had told the warriors that a pair resembling them matched the ones I had been seen wearing. When my mother was confronted, she refused to acknowledge any existence of them or me. In her persistent denial and the warriors accusations of them possibly being stolen, since no reclaimed owned anything nice or were worthy of moccasins containing beading, the argument had caused my mother's heart to fail, and she died.

My aunt Mayma was devastated and said that I had fled the camp with my son in tow. She was in fear of some Spirit taking her as they just had my mother right in front of her that she was afraid to keep silent. She wouldn't say if they were the same moccasins just that I had some that were beaded once. They had inquired as to where I had stolen them from, and where they would find me. My Aunt claimed she knew nothing of where the moccasins came from, only that I had fled to the hills and would say no more. I felt a bit of relief, yet saw the hesitancy in her stare as she finished relaying this to me got up and went to pour more water into a cup and drank it.

She said nothing more to me as we sat there most of the day, sweating from the heat and no flow of air coming in since the front flap of the entrance to the tipi was kept closed. I supposed it was a punishment for me, and felt sad that she had to feel the stifling warmth building up, although she could get up and leave often. I could not. I was even lowered to having to use the bathroom in an old clay jug, because I was to go nowhere.

At least I was now allowed to walk around the tipi, as long as I stayed away from the entrance. I think that was because it was clearly evident that I would not go anywhere without my son, and they made sure my only contact with him was when they allowed it and I was at the farthest point from my only escape, and them between me and that means of escape.

The women mentioned nothing more about what the search uncovered when they came into our camp. I knew nothing more of what my aunt or momma had told them or what was known by the elders or the council. I certainly was not going to ask them and draw any suspicion.

I kept quiet and did as I was told the two miserable days I was forced to stay there. I tried to stay close to my son and tend to his every need and hope that no one noticed the birthmark on his thigh that would give away his legacy. It was much easier to play the idiot half-blood until I knew how much had actually been revealed. Besides, I was wearing an old pair of moccasins that were my aunts, and had buried the ones halfway along the way to where I rested among the trees.

~

Just then the flap door of the tipi opened and in stomped Alisais' youngest cousin WanyaKe.

My heart began to pound as he grabbed my arm with such force, shaking me awake from my heat exhausted nap. I had been resting with Little Bird when, he tumbled onto the bedding and WanyaKe motioned for one of the women to grab him and bring him along as well.

Cursing as he pulled me out the entry and up the short path to the tribal council tipi. I cried out, "my son, my son, let me carry my son!" He motioned and ordered for her to bring him to me, so I would stop screaming and continued pulling me by the arm to face the council.

I was ushered in and forced to sit down on the floor between two elders and directly across from Alisais and his father. The Chief looked at me as if he wanted to cut my heart out and feed it to the vultures, while Alisais sat there silently, looking down making no eye contact with anyone. Deep down inside, despite my fear, I felt compassion and desire. I wanted to reach out and touch him, comfort him, and couldn't.

It was silent for a few minutes and I started to feel a bit of panic overcome me. My thoughts began to race around in my head as if to be a wolf on a circular hunt around the moon. To my knowledge, never was a half-blood ever called before the council and it ever turned out good. It always meant they did something horrid enough to be banished, whipped or put to death. There was no evidence of the moccasins on me. No one had seen the mark on my sons thigh.

Why was I being treated so harshly?

Had I been called here to stand before them and be punished for disgracing my mother because I was off in the woods, and not at her side at her passing? They didn't care much for any of us, so why did it matter?

What was going to happen to me?

What did they know?

Had the council decided that those half-bloods still remaining in camp be eliminated, as we had heard rumor of happening when they came of age in other camps and they would take my son from me?

Had our dying Chief put pressure on Alisais to take more control and eliminate any traces of the white man's world as retaliation for the burning hatred that festered following the recent months raids by soldiers, taking the lives of nearly half of our people?

Surely this had more to do with me than just disgracing my mother and our customs for the dying!

What was it?

My head swam in a state of confusion and fright. That moment Alisais raised his gaze and our eyes locked. He gasped. Immediately standing up, he tore away the covering I had placed over my son, looked at me, and with the speed of a jaguar he fled out of the tipi.

They knew....

The Beaded Moccasins belonged to me...

JENAI DAWN

Epilogue

Still rattled and frightened of her future, and at the behest of Alisais, she was to be confined to a small tipi with her son, while the council decided her fate.

They knew the moccasins were hers!

They knew that through deceit, she had conceived Alisais' child, a son, and the firstborn of the future leader of the people.

Unsure of anything to come, she was resolved to try and make the best of her situation. As she settled into the small tipi, with her son, she found happiness and a small sense of comfort knowing that they would be together for now.

Under constant guard, but alive, she still had her dreams, her hopes and the love of her son. Emmalia also had the memories and promise that one day, "She will find acceptance among many and her son shall bring their people to greatness" as her mother had often said that the Sprits predicted.

Pained that the man she had grown to love while caring for her sister and sought her out, now probably hated her as much as his father, the Chief, did. Time stood still as days passed and her fate was left unknown to her. Despite the harshness of Alisais' families tribal traditions, she held in her heart a silent prayer that he would have more mercy than his father.

Wishing that one day he would find forgiveness, find the love he once showed for her, make her his wife, and love her and his son as he did Laylah. For now she, would find solace in being alive and holding her most cherished treasure, Little Bird, in her arms.

If you enjoyed this book;

Be sure to check out other books in the Beaded Moccasin Chronicles.

Emma's Hope: (Book 2) Takes you along with Emma and Little Bird as they struggle with their new life among the main tribe along the banks of Pagoda Creek in the war-torn prairies of Pigeon Gap, Kansas. Spring 2015

Reclamation: (Book 3) Summer 2015.

With Eagles Wings: (Book 4) Fall 2015